For Ali
Best wishes
Paulie
(P.R.Page)

Simon's
Fel

Simon's Fel

P. R. Page

Matador
9 Priory Business Park
Kibworth Beauchamp
Leicestershire LE8 0RX, UK
Tel: (+44) 116 279 2299
Fax: (+44) 116 279 2277
Email: books@troubador.co.uk
Web: www.troubador.co.uk/matador

ISBN 978-1784620-035

British Library Cataloguing in Publication Data.
A catalogue record for this book is available from the British Library.

Typeset in Palatino by Troubador Publishing Ltd
Printed and bound in the UK by TJ International, Padstow, Cornwall

Matador is an imprint of Troubador Publishing Ltd

For Roger Hayes:

My first love;
Lost to me for so long, but now found.
My inspiration for this book.
He has made me so incredibly happy.
My love to him and for him always.

One

Lissy woke and turned her head to look at the clock; it was ten to five in the morning. She hadn't woken that early for months, it was then she remembered she'd been so exhausted last night, she had gone to bed without any sleeping pills. She lay there for a few moments then got out of bed and went to the window. The bedroom was on the third floor of the townhouse and she could see the whole street to the traffic lights at the top of the hill. Her eyes riveted on the lights and she drew her breath in sharply, waiting for the dreadful wave of panic and guilt to wash over her. It didn't happen! She exhaled slowly and lowered her gaze, then raised it again and once more focussed on the traffic lights; nothing; no reaction. She smiled, her face coming alight, her breathing calm and even. The sense of relief and release from two years of anguish and guilt was intensely liberating. She was free, after all this time, she was free!

She stared out of the window again and took in the whole scene below her, looking at it through newly opened eyes. People were hurrying along, the street was already crowded and it was still so early in the morning. The rumble of the traffic got louder as more and more vehicles appeared on the busy road. Lorries and vans were jostling for space to drop off their loads and there was a constant hum of voices and traffic. It was all so hectic, so crowded and the noise assailed her ears. She had never got used to the constant buzz and hum of this London suburb. Lissy sighed deeply and turned to look at the clock again. She had been standing there for half an hour just taking in her surroundings. She hated everything about this place, the house, the location and the never ending noise. What on earth was she doing here? The question shot into her mind and like a flash of lightning the answer came to her.

Abruptly, she turned round, ran into the hallway and entered the room which had been her husband's study. She hadn't been in there for nearly two years, not since he had died. But today she had a purpose. She dragged open the doors of the huge wooden cabinet which dominated the room and quickly searched through the drawers. Most were empty but she knew the item she was looking for was there somewhere. Her mother had cleared all the glossy magazines and books from the sitting room before his funeral and had put them in the cabinet. Out of the way she had stated, as it was not 'seemly' to have them around at such a time. Smiling as she found the magazine, excitement coursing through her veins, Lissy went into the kitchen and leafed through the pages until she found it. This was it! The advert for the cottage, this was where she should be! She made herself a cup of tea, sat at the small bistro table in the kitchen and gazed at the picture in the magazine, an idea forming in her mind. Could she do this? Would she have the courage to see it through? Her excitement and resolve increased as the idea grew in her mind. She took a deep breath and gathered her whirling thoughts. She gazed round the kitchen, taking stock of her surroundings. For two years she had been locked in a prison of unhappiness, then guilt and remorse, but now she was free of all that, her life was her own. Smiling happily, she searched for a pen and some paper and began to make her plans.

Two

It didn't take Lissy long to put her plans in place. She gathered together the papers she had written and sat back in her chair reflecting on the events that had changed her life so suddenly overnight. *Get busy living or get busy dying.* The phrase stood out in her mind. The main character in the film she had watched last night, *Shawshank Redemption,* had said it shortly before he escaped from Shawshank prison, innocent of the crime of which he had been convicted. She would do just the same. Escape from her self-imposed prison and get busy living.

Galvanised into action by this thought, she decided her first task was to get her possessions from the attic. She opened the hatch, lowered the ladder, climbed into the loft and found the bags holding her old familiar clothes that had been discarded by her husband as 'unsuitable'. He had instructed her to get rid of them but she had bagged them up and put them in the attic while he was at work. She'd discovered very early in her marriage not to argue or disagree with him when he became so domineering. Occasionally she would rebel, but only when he was not at home. She threw the bags onto the landing and climbed down from the attic. She emptied the bags onto the bedroom floor; the clothes were musty and smelt of mothballs, but they were hers. She sorted through them and decided to keep them all. They would be her whole wardrobe until she shopped for more when she arrived at her destination. She kept out smart blue jeans and a denim shirt to wear later for her journey.

Lissy returned to the attic and collected together the boxes that held her art and craft equipment. These too had been packed away as they were deemed 'unnecessary' for her new position in life as the wife of a lawyer, soon to become a barrister. Her budding career as an art and drama teacher had been stopped almost before it began. Her husband had been horrified that she even contemplated working. She carefully re-packed all her tools and books into the boxes, then stacked them on the landing. Finally she fetched two suitcases from the loft, packed her clothes and personal belongings and put these beside the boxes on the landing. Two suitcases and four boxes; not a great deal to show for twenty-five years.

It had taken her almost three hours to complete this task. She looked round the townhouse, there was nothing else she wanted or needed to take with her. Nothing else here was hers, not even the designer clothes hanging in the wardrobe. Nothing had been her choice, everything had been bought by her husband. *Late husband*, she corrected herself under her breath.

Bringing her thoughts back to her next task, Lissy took a deep breath, dialled her mother's number and waited for her to answer the phone. As soon as she had said hello, Lissy quickly informed her mother she was going away for a while and would call her when she reached her destination. Her mother, horrified at Lissy's news launched into a tirade, trying to dissuade her from embarking on what she considered nonsensical action.

"You can't Lissy, you can't go away, you are not well enough, you need help, it's too soon. I will come and stay with you." Her mother's voice was rising in horror and anger at her daughter's news. "This is nonsense," she continued, "you don't know what you are doing, you cannot make decisions like this for yourself."

Lissy cut her short saying "I'm going, I will contact you when I get there." She ended the call smiling at herself and pleased that at last, for the first time in twenty-five years, she had stood up to her mother and made her own decision. She showered and dressed, her old familiar jeans and denim shirt feeling good against her skin. Smiling widely she made her way down to the basement garages where Peter, the young mechanic employed there to look after the resident's vehicles, greeted her with a warm smile.

"Mornin Mrs H, haven't seen you in a long while. Need the four by four do you? It's all tanked up and running nicely. Goin somewhere?" Lissy nodded and smiling back at him asked if he would fetch the suitcases and boxes from the house and load them into the car as she would be leaving in about an hour and wouldn't be coming back. Having made this statement which caused

Peter's mouth to drop open, she handed him the house keys and went off to the local estate agent clutching her precious magazine and the sheaf of papers.

Three

Lissy walked into the estate agents' office just after ten o'clock and Mr Riley, the owner, greeted her warmly; he hadn't seen her since her husband had died. She looked well, he thought, but wondered what had brought her here after nearly two years? He had been involved with settling the will as far as the property was concerned, and had sent all the information to the solicitor. Subsequently he was informed by them that it was finalised and that new deeds showing Mrs Huntley-James as the sole owner would be sent to him for safe keeping. Apparently, that instruction had come from Mrs Huntley-James, she had expressed no wish to deal with any of the administration.

"How can I help you Mrs Huntley-James? Is there a problem with your property?" Mr Riley had settled himself behind his desk, intrigued at what could be the reason was for this visit. Lissy smiled and handed over the sheaf of papers with all her instructions neatly written on the four pages.

"Please read through these papers Mr Riley, I will answer any questions you may have but those instructions must be adhered to without any change or deviation. I would like this dealt with as soon as possible, it is imperative that it is finalised without delay." She stopped and waited while Mr Riley scanned the pages.

His eyebrows rose as he read on, but he didn't speak until he had reached the end. Sighing, he put the papers down and looked at Lissy.

"Are you really serious about this? Are you sure you want to sell up and move?" His manner was stern and fatherly.

"My decision is final. In future, please refer to me as Miss Huntley."

"Of course my dear, as you wish." Mr Riley shuffled in his seat, cleared his throat, leant on his desk and smiled. "I think I may have a solution, strange as it may seem but I know someone who has been waiting for one of those townhouses to become vacant. His name is Alexander Gossington and he has been an Associate of this firm for nearly a year. He is in rented property at the moment, I am sure he will jump at the chance to purchase your townhouse. I will go and ask him to join us, excuse me for a moment." Mr Riley left his office and Lissy couldn't quite believe what she had just heard, it seemed as though luck was on her side at last.

Mr Riley returned accompanied by a tall, good looking man, very confident in his manner and suave in his appearance. Introductions were made, and they spent the next hour discussing the townhouse, its contents and just how soon they could finalise the deal. Alexander was extremely pleased as he walked past the townhouses each morning on his way to the office, and had been patiently waiting for one to come on the market. He had the money in the bank, an inheritance from his grandfather, so was in a position to purchase immediately. He was happy to buy it as it was including all the furniture and fittings. Lissy was amused when he said he could dispose of the clothes she was leaving behind, his girlfriend might even like some! Agreement was reached on the final price, and Alexander also consented to pay any legal expenses that may arise over and above their normal fees. Lissy had secured a promise that her post would be collected by them and when she had arrived at her destination, she would inform Mr Riley where to send it. Satisfied that everything was sorted between them, the secretary was summoned to type out their agreement.

Mr Riley however, was concerned that this agreement had not been fully discussed. He pointed out the pitfalls that could arise without surveys being completed. He was astonished that Alexander, normally extremely businesslike in his negotiations, had agreed so readily to purchase the townhouse. He was unaware just how much he coveted one of these very desirable properties. Alexander in turn, assured his boss that no surveys were required as he'd done a great deal of research on the properties, preparing for an opportunity such as this to buy one. Lissy reminded Mr Riley of the instructions she had given him. Her decision was final.

Mr Riley sighed and shook his head at what he considered to be the somewhat rash decision these two were making. He sighed again and summoned his secretary to bring the typed papers. Both smiling hugely at their good luck, Lissy and Alexander duly signed the documents witnessed by Mr Riley and his very efficient secretary.

It was now approaching midday and Lissy wanted to be on her way, so she stood up, said her goodbyes and left the office. If Mr Riley needed her he could always phone her on her mobile. She had her agreement in writing, nothing else was needed, she could go. She made her way to the bank to pay in the Bank Draft for £650,000, the agreed final sum for the sale of her townhouse. She ignored all the advice that the teller tried to give her about investing it, just smiled and went on her way to the newsagents. There she bought a road atlas, some simple supplies for her journey and went back to the townhouse. A quick look round confirmed in her mind that there was nothing else she needed, her luggage and boxes had been collected by Peter, so she locked the door and went to the garage. Peter was waiting for her. She thanked him for his help, passed over a £20 note and handed him the bunch of house keys asking if he would take them to Mr Riley. Smiling happily at her generosity, he readily agreed, gave her a cheeky peck on the cheek, wished her a happy journey and went on his way.

Lissy stood looking at the four by four for several minutes, it was a long time since she had driven. Would she have the confidence to drive so far? She shook herself, pushing away her doubts and climbed into the driving seat. After a few moments of familiarising herself with the controls, she started the engine and moved slowly out of the garage and onto the road. Happily smiling now that she was on her way, she realised she was hungry. She would stop at a pub she knew just out of town; she'd been there a few times with friends from college. Putting aside the thought that it could have changed completely from what she remembered, she decided to take a chance and stop there for lunch.

The pub had changed hands, but she was welcomed and shown to a small table tucked in the corner of the restaurant where she could be private but comfortable. As she ate her lunch, she studied the map and worked out a route for her journey. She had no real idea of how long it would take or exactly how far it was. She just knew with absolute certainty that she had to get out of London and head west to start her new life.

Four

The waitress brought coffee and Lissy thanked her as she took the cup and made her way into the small lounge. She settled back in a chair, opened the magazine and gazed at the cottage that had caught her attention, oh so long ago. She had hidden the magazine from her husband, knowing he would never have contemplated living in such a property or indeed in such a place. He was too entrenched in city life, his business was in the City and he had no thought for anything or anyone that wouldn't be conducive to his way of life. The cottage had become the symbol of her ideal place to live and she had dreamed of it for a long time. After her husband had died, she often thought about the cottage wondering if she would ever get an opportunity to live in such a beautiful place. She had not looked at the magazine for the last two years since her mother had scooped it up amongst others from the table the day her husband had been buried. She had put them in the cabinet in his office, knowing full well that her daughter would not venture in there. Her husband had made sure that Lissy understood it was his domain and his alone. Lissy's mother considered her daughter's interest in the cottage to be irrelevant and a pipe dream, therefore of no consequence whatsoever.

When she and Lissy's husband had met, it became obvious very quickly that they were two of a kind. Both were ambitious, ruthless, mentally cruel, extremely self-centred and very selfish. They had immediately become friends and between them made Lissy's life a complete misery. They had dominated her and consequently she had completely lost her confidence. At last that was all over, it had taken nearly two years but now she was free and could live her life as she wanted. Yes, she was scared, her confidence still fragile, but her resolve was sure, she knew where she was going, where she wanted to be. She sat up, gathered her papers and her bag then purposefully made her way back to her car, intent on reaching her destination without further delay.

The small village she was heading for was in the West Country, in the heart of Devon, close to the moors though not completely isolated. She had worked out it would take her around four or five hours to drive there, so she decided to stop when she was about halfway to phone the estate agent advertising the cottage. She wouldn't allow herself to think that it may no longer be available. She pushed away the nagging doubts that rose in her thoughts. If it was sold, she'd cross that bridge when she came to it, she had no idea what she'd do. Pushing away the pessimism, she determinedly drove on.

Lissy decided as she drove along that she would drop her nickname, she'd always disliked it. Her mother and husband had started to call her Lissy, telling her it was 'fashionable' to create one from your own name. From now on she would revert to her maiden name, Felicity Huntley. After all, she reasoned, she was no longer married, she was widowed, therefore she didn't have to use her married name. It was quite the fashion for women to retain their maiden names even when married. She felt relaxed and happy with this decision; it seemed the natural thing to do in her new found freedom.

After driving for a couple of hours, keeping an eye on the map and enjoying the lovely countryside along the way, she stopped in a small town just inside the Dorset border and with trembling fingers, called the estate agent. The man who answered sounded elderly and was helpful and reassuring. The property was still on the market as it required a great deal of work to make it habitable and no-one seemed to want to take on the task. Excited that her dream home was still for sale, Felicity asked when she could view it; she wouldn't be arriving until around 6 pm. No problem the agent had replied, he lived above the office and if she rang the bell on his apartment door, he would gladly show her round the cottage. Thanking him profusely, she gave him her name and mobile number and agreed to meet him at 6 pm. As she drove off again she realised she hadn't asked his name, she was too excited.

As she got closer, Felicity was imagining herself in her cottage garden planting and picking the wild flowers and herbs, making her collages and herbal infusions and just anything else she could think of. She started singing, something she hadn't done in years. She was happy, free and coming alive again.

Five

Felicity arrived in the village just after six o'clock. It was small, the cottages set back from the road, the spire of a church towering above the roofs. It all looked so pretty in the early evening sunshine. She was somewhat of a realist and knew she was looking at it through rose tinted glasses, but she immediately felt at home, as though she was always meant to be here. Well, it *would* be her home, she *was* here, and here to stay. She knew before she had even seen it that she was going to buy the cottage.

She climbed stiffly out of the car, not used to driving long distances. She stretched luxuriously and heard a voice calling to her from across the road. A small round man with a delightful smile and a shock of white hair was waving at her. He strode across the road, took her hand and shook it vigorously saying:

"Welcome Mrs Huntley, my name is Ray Luxton. I hope your drive from London was pleasant." Immediately, Felicity corrected him.

"I am Miss Huntley," she said, "Felicity Huntley."

"Of course my dear, are you ready to view the cottage? Please follow me." An observant and sensitive man, he'd noticed she was wearing a wedding ring and it intrigued him; divorced or widowed he wondered? He turned and walked away so Felicity grabbed her bag from the car, quickly locked it and hurried after him. He had gone about a hundred metres and had seemingly disappeared in a hedge across the road. As Felicity approached, he was standing by a rickety gate a few metres from the road. He grinned at her as she stopped dead, her eyes shining and a huge smile lighting up her face. Ray Luxton's heart flipped, he hadn't seen such joy on a woman's face for a long, long time. He felt tears well in his eyes and he took an instant liking to this lovely young woman. He felt fiercely protective of her; she looked so vulnerable. He wanted to take her in his arms and hug her and enjoy this moment with her, obviously so momentous to her.

Restraining himself, surprised also at his immediate reaction to her, he settled for offering her his arm to lead her to the cottage. Touched by his kindness, Felicity put her arm through his, her own mind registering that she felt an instant liking and respect for this dear man. Smiling together like long lost friends, they walked round to the side of the cottage through the overgrown garden. Ray let go of Felicity and wrestled first with the key and then with the door to get it open. It suddenly yielded to his efforts and flew open, Ray almost falling in with it. Laughing, he turned and beckoned her in.

"This is the kitchen, a good size but it needs

modernising and..." He stopped as Felicity interrupted him,

"Mr Luxton, please don't say any more, you don't have to try to sell the cottage to me, I am going to buy it. I have wanted it for years, nothing and no-one will stop me from being here, I belong in this cottage." She smiled again, her eyes filling with tears, she was so happy and overwhelmed with the sense of belonging that she felt. Ray went towards her and then hugged her to him. She cried on his shoulder, tears of release, peace and happiness. He shed a few tears himself, overcome by how this young woman had come to this place and taken it to her heart. Suddenly she started to laugh, extricated herself from Ray's bear hug and asked him how much the vendors wanted for the cottage.

"Well," Ray said, "because it needs so much doing, the asking price is £55,000, but the owner will take £50,000 as he wants rid of it. It has been empty for over two years since the old lady who previously owned it died, and the family don't want it."

"Can I buy it now?" Felicity asked, "I have the funds for a cash purchase from the sale of my previous property. I want to move in straight away as I have nowhere else to go." Somewhat taken aback at this instant decision by Felicity, Ray hesitated, then said:

"We can sort out the legalities tomorrow my dear, but I will get a SOLD board from my office and put it up now. If you change your mind, we can always remove it. You have a look round, but be careful, the stairs aren't too sound and if you wander round the garden, take care you don't trip over a rabbit or fox or badger hole, they are probably all about the garden somewhere. I will also pop into the pub round the corner, they have B & B accommodation. Would you like me to book a room for you?"

Felicity nodded at Ray, realising she would need somewhere to stay for a few days.

Ray continued, "I will book you in there and after we have done here, you must join me for dinner. I am eating there tonight and please call me Ray." He smiled hugely at Felicity and went out quickly, his heart fluttering as he dashed along the road.

Felicity smiled again and threw her hands in the air, danced around the kitchen and sang happily as she explored the rooms. The kitchen was indeed large and there were two smaller rooms leading from it, one dominated by a huge sink against the wall. She reasoned the cottage must have been some sort of farm building. Opposite the kitchen were two more rooms, both quite large and with French doors leading out to the garden. The doors were locked and she couldn't see the extent of the garden as it was so overgrown. Back in the kitchen she went through the door at one end which led through to a hallway and the boarded up front door. A staircase was to one side and with some trepidation she ventured up. The stairs creaked and groaned under her feet but held firm. There were three bedrooms and a bathroom, devoid of a bath and sink, just an ancient toilet with an overhead cistern. She went back to the bedrooms and looked in each one, all three had a fireplace. The windows were cracked and dirty, the floorboards uneven and unpolished, and there were some odd bits of furniture but no beds.

Descending to the hallway, Felicity closed her eyes and imagined how it could be renovated. She was so engrossed with her thoughts that she didn't hear the man come in. He was standing by the kitchen door glaring at her. A sudden noise startled her and she opened her eyes to see a white shadow dash past the window.

"Felicity, Felicity, where are you?" Ray was calling her. She quickly went into the kitchen, glad to see him, the shadow she had seen receding from her thoughts when she saw the SOLD board in Ray's hand and a hammer in the other.

"Come and help me put this up on the gate post and then we'll go to dinner. I have booked you the very best room at the pub for an indefinite period, so you now have somewhere to go."

He beamed at her and together they went out, secured the SOLD sign, remembered to lock the kitchen door and went arm in arm to the pub.

Six

After a delightful dinner, they sat together in the snug bar with coffee and brandy. Ray had insisted dinner was his treat, and he had introduced Felicity to his sister Lucy and brother-in-law Michael, the landlords of the Trenchard Tavern. Their son Justin, currently spending a few days at home from university, had fetched her luggage and boxes from her car and taken them all to her room.

It had been a very eventful day, she was more tired than she realised. She'd sold a house and then bought a cottage, all in one day. Coupled with the long drive and the emotional trauma, she was exhausted but she was happy. She hadn't felt that way for a very long time.

Felicity sighed, leant back in her chair and smiled at her new friend. They had chatted amiably over dinner and Ray had told her his wife had died a few years previously. Subsequently, he had sold their home and bought this small estate agency, something to keep him busy and occupied. He was a very young fifty-eight years old, too young to retire, lonely after he lost his wife. They had no children so he really was alone. Lucy and Michael had encouraged him in his idea to buy the business in Little Trenchard, the accommodation above the office was lovely and really comfortable. He'd been here now for almost five years and was very happy in his life. Felicity sensed he was curious about her own circumstances, but even her new found freedom couldn't bring her to open the locked box in her mind that contained the dreadful memories of the last three years of her life. She just briefly told Ray that she'd been about to start her teaching career in art, craft, drama and music but had met and married a very successful lawyer, due to become a barrister. They had moved to a fashionable area on the outskirts of London where she'd remained until today. Taking a deep breath, she finished by stating flatly and coldly that her husband had died in a serious road accident. They'd been married just over a year. She was nervously twisting her wedding ring round and round on her finger, her hands shaking as she related this to Ray. He had noticed this and also the change of expression on her face. She had been scared of this man he thought, he could almost feel her fear as she spoke of him. All vivacity had drained from her and she looked frightened.

As he leant forward wanting to reassure her, the door from the street opened and a tall, rugged man with sandy hair wearing jeans and a white shirt came in. Felicity's eyes opened wide. A white shirt? Surely not, it couldn't have been this man she'd seen passing the window at the cottage, the place had been deserted. Her eyes met his.

They were dark eyes, not brown, just dark. They pierced deep into her soul. She inhaled sharply and stopped breathing, unable to move. He held her gaze for what seemed an age, then abruptly he turned towards Ray and demanded to know why a SOLD board was attached to the gate of the cottage.

"Because Simon," Ray replied quietly, "the cottage has been sold and this is the new owner, Felicity Huntley." Slowly, the man identified as Simon turned his gaze back to Felicity, once more she felt frozen until he tore his eyes away from hers.

"Why did you sell it Ray? You knew I wanted it!" He threw the question at Ray, anger in his voice. He was visibly trembling, obviously trying to control his feelings.

"You are well aware of the answer to that question Simon, we've had this conversation before. The cottage is now sold and that is the end of the matter."

Ray turned away from Simon, dismissal in his gesture. He had seen all the nuances and reactions that had occurred over the last few minutes between these two people, and it intrigued him greatly. This woman had depths, yet to be explored. What was he thinking of? Not for himself, but Simon? Now why on earth should he think that? He hardly knew Felicity but felt as though he knew her well. He shook his head, he was getting fanciful. But Simon? He had never seen him so pent up and like a rocket about to explode. Felicity had made a huge impact on Simon; just why Ray didn't know and after just one brief meeting! No words had been exchanged between them, but the tension was almost palpable. He'd known

Simon for a few years and respected him greatly, but this was a side of him Ray hadn't seen before. He could see fireworks ahead. He looked up and saw Lucy serving Simon who had moved away to the bar. She too had noticed the tensions between these two young people and the impact they had on each other. She raised her eyebrows at Ray in acknowledgement of what they had both observed.

Life in Little Trenchard was about to change.

Seven

Felicity went down next morning for breakfast to find she was the only one in the dining room. The other guests had been up early and gone off to explore the moors. Lucy explained this to Felicity as she brought the food she'd ordered. They chatted amiably, both enjoying the chance to have a quiet chat. Lucy was intrigued by this young woman, and could fully understand why Ray had taken to her.

Suddenly realising the time, Lucy sent Felicity off to see Ray to prepare the documents for buying the cottage and to pick up the keys to her new home. After much discussion and explanation from Ray regarding the legalities of the purchase she signed her name on the papers. It was relatively straightforward as the owner wanted to be rid of it and Felicity was adamant she wanted it no matter the condition. Ray would pass the papers on to the owner's solicitor for their signature. Felicity, thrilled that the legal papers had been completed, wrote out a cheque for £50,000 which she handed to Ray to pass on along with the papers he was sending to the owner's solicitor. In return, he handed her the keys to her cottage. He was once more struck by the complete look of joy and happiness that washed over her face as she left the office clutching the keys tightly in her hand. Ever observant, Ray noticed that Felicity had removed her wedding ring. He wondered what it was that had made her do this. Once more he felt intrigued about her; she really was an interesting person.

Felicity went straight to the cottage, determined to have a good look round, take measurements and make notes of the work that would need doing to make her cottage habitable and turn it into the home she had dreamed of for so long. She was undaunted by the magnitude of the job involved, and didn't care how long it took; it had to be right. Humming to herself, she took the tape measure, pad and pencil from her bag and started her task. She would measure each room and make notes as she went along. Ideas were already forming in her mind, visions of what it could look like started to take root.

She was so engrossed in her task, she didn't see or hear Simon come in. He stood quietly watching her for a few moments as she crawled around the kitchen floor with the tape. She exclaimed loudly as she banged her head under the sink. Backing out, she sat on the floor brushing cobwebs from her hair. She suddenly became aware of a pair of boots in her line of sight and let out a peal of laughter at the absurdity of the situation. Without thinking Simon held out a hand to help Felicity up. She looked up at him as she took his proffered hand, he was smiling and laughing with her. Another sharp intake of breath caught at her chest. When he smiled his eyes were beautiful, smoky grey with silver specks. Entranced, she stood there her hand still in his, then she stumbled back as he suddenly let go, the moment gone but not forgotten.

"Can I help you with the tape, it's easier with two?" Simon took the tape from her hand without waiting for her to answer, then proceeded to instruct her where to place it as they went from room to room taking measurements. No words were spoken apart from his curt instructions. She was acutely aware of his presence; he unnerved her, but without menace. An hour later, all the rooms measured, he left as abruptly as he had come. She ran her fingers through her hair, surprised that they were shaking. She sat down on the floor before her knees buckled, her legs unsteady. Why did he have such an effect on her? She must ask Lucy and Michael about Simon. But why? Why did she need to know anything about him? Why this interest in a man she hardly knew? She didn't want to get involved again, it only brought pain and heartache. She didn't want to think about the impact he had on her. Why hadn't it worried her that a comparative stranger had let himself into her cottage? All this ran through her mind confusing her. She shook her head to rid herself of these unwelcome and disturbing thoughts.

Felicity went into the garden and Simon watched her from the shelter of the trees. She had got under his skin.

She shouldn't be here. He wanted the cottage but she had got it. He didn't have the money to buy it but he was so sure that by right it should be his. How could he get her away until he found out the truth? He continued to watch her as she wandered around, noticing how the sunlight sparkled off the red glints in her auburn hair, the freckles on her face prominent when she turned her face into the sun. What was the matter with him? He should be hating her, she had his cottage. He found himself feeling jealous of the fact that he'd seen Ray with his arms around her and of how much he wished it had been him. He shook himself, angry at the road his thoughts were taking. Damn the woman, why had she come here?

Eight

Ray had taken Felicity under his wing and suggested he help her to find a reliable builder for the massive task of renovating her cottage. She was more than happy to let him do this as she had absolutely no knowledge of the building trade or of trustworthy local builders. With the assistance of Lucy and Michael, and his local knowledge after living in the area for some while, he employed Abe Bresland, a local independent builder with excellent references. Ray had got to know him shortly after he had taken over the estate agency. Abe had called in to introduce himself and to ask Ray to keep some of his business cards for anyone to use if they needed any work done. He worked mostly locally and was well liked as a good, dependable builder. Ray asked Felicity along to the office to meet him and discuss her plans. Abe Bresland was fifty years old, tall and wiry with a very pleasant personality. He'd been known as Abe since his schooldays, no-one remembered what his name actually was. His initials, A.B, had turned into Abe, and even his wife called him that.

Felicity liked him, he was calm and reassuring and took time over her plans. He discussed with her the changes necessary when it involved drains, pipe-work and electrical circuits. He smiled at her and explained some of it would have to be decided in situ, as no plans of the drainage and suchlike seemed to be available. He currently employed two young men, Stan and Dave, as labourers. He was also training them in other skills while they worked on his projects. Abe was a qualified electrician and plumber, proficient in the skills of carpentry and brickwork. He could fit windows, build staircases. In fact, he could probably build a whole house himself. Felicity was delighted, and she felt she could trust him and leave him to get on with the work, knowing he would follow her plans. Terms settled, Abe agreed to start the following week, estimating he could complete the work in three or four months as the whole team would be concentrating on just her cottage. He assured Felicity that both Stan and Dave were trustworthy young men and would work hard alongside him to adhere to her requirements. He would take over completely, managing the whole project. She could come along at any time she wanted to see how they were progressing. He left her some bathroom and kitchen catalogues to browse through and once she had made up her mind, she must let him know her choices and he would do the rest.

Abe Bresland went on his way, excited at this quite complicated job. Pleased he had been awarded the contract, he'd quietly thanked Ray for recommending him. He went home to study the plans and make the calls to his suppliers for the materials he would need to start the following week. His young wife, Jeannie, would be pleased to know there was another young woman in the village. She was twenty years younger than Abe, and had few friends as the majority of the people in the village were over fifty. They had two young children of whom he was inordinately proud. He had met Jeannie just three years before when he had literally bumped into her at a bank in Plymouth. He had picked her up from the pavement, appalled that he had knocked her over. She had smiled at him assuring him she was alright and turned to go, but impulsively he had asked her to join him for a coffee to recover from her shock. She had readily agreed and that had been the beginning of a whirlwind courtship. They had married just four months later and were blissfully happy. He knew she would like Felicity, such a pleasant young woman; it would be good for her to have a friend in the village. He was smiling as he went into their house, greeted his wife with a bear hug and lingering kiss and still holding her hand, proceeded to tell her his news.

Happy that the work on her cottage was to start so soon, Felicity turned her thoughts to her arts and craft. Perhaps there would be a local market for her to sell them; she could set up a small cottage business. Excited with this idea, she spent considerable time around the area, picking wild flowers and herbs, taking photographs of local scenes and people. Back in her room at the pub, she realised she had nowhere to keep them so she went down to the kitchen and asked Lucy if she could have some vases and pots to keep her wild flowers and herbs in. Intrigued, Lucy asked what she was doing with them all, so Felicity fetched her portfolio of her previous work and showed it to Lucy.

Fascinated, Lucy spent some time leafing through the portfolio. She was impressed with Felicity's obvious talent and after consulting with Michael, asked Felicity to produce some paintings and collages for the pub, their bed and breakfast rooms and for their own accommodation. Delighted, Felicity insisted they would be a gift to thank them both for making her so welcome and comfortable. She was so insistent that Lucy finally agreed. However, she determined to talk with Michael later and think of something special to give to Felicity when the cottage was finished. Happy with these decisions, it was not long before Felicity had produced several items for Lucy and Michael.

The first two of Felicity's paintings had only been on display for two days when several customers asked Lucy if she knew the artist and were they for sale. Excited for Felicity, Lucy told the customers that she actually was a guest at the pub, and she would pass the enquiries on to her. Lucy suggested Felicity leave her portfolio behind the bar, customers could then see more of her work. Soon she was receiving commissions from visitors to the pub; her business was on its way! She couldn't believe that only five weeks had passed since she had left London. She would need to find a workshop and soon, she couldn't continue to work in the confines of her room at the pub. This prompted her to see Ray and task him to find a small office or studio that she could turn into her craft workshop. Her life had taken a huge turn for the better, she had her cottage, she would be self-sufficient and best of all, she was happy.

Nine

Ray diligently took on the task of finding a studio for Felicity. A couple of days later, he took her to see the small place he had found in the next village, Middle Trenchard, just a few miles away. It was located above the garage in the village, and had private access both at the front and rear. The studio had all the facilities that Felicity would need for her project and it was completely self-contained. There were several windows that gave excellent light, and two large skylights added to the feeling of airiness and space. It was just what Felicity needed, and would give her the opportunity to arrange craft classes and workshops as there was plenty of space. All she needed to fully equip the studio would be some workstations, worktops and shelving. Happy with the studio, she thanked Ray and they went back to the pub to have lunch together and then to Ray's office to complete the rental papers.

Felicity spent the next couple of days shopping for work stations; she needed these to be mobile and individual. At a large office furniture retailer in Plymouth, she found exactly what she wanted. They were basically computer desks, on wheels with melamine tops, eminently suitable for painting and craft work and easily cleaned. To one side, built in under the desktop were drawers with a pull-out tray set in above the drawers. Pens, pencils and brushes could all be laid out on these trays, just what she had envisaged. To her delight, in the same style, there was a double desk almost twice the length with drawer units at either end. This was just what she needed to do her own work. Deciding that six of the smaller ones would be a good number to start with, plus the one she required, the order was placed and delivery arranged for two days later.

Driving back to the pub, she was pondering with a slight frown how she would get these flat pack workstations put together, plus who on earth could she ask to erect the worktops and shelves she needed? Abe couldn't spare either Stan or Dave, they were fully occupied with renovating her cottage. She sighed and decided she would ask Lucy and Michael, they may know of someone local who could do this for her. She was back at Little Trenchard when she spotted Simon halfway up a ladder, busy fitting windows into the new classroom at the school. She braked suddenly, leapt out of the car and before she could stop to think, she approached Simon and blurted out that she had a job for him if he was interested. She put her shaking hands into the pockets of her jeans and waited for his answer, her eyes riveted on the bottom of the ladder.

"Me?" he asked in total surprise at her sudden approach. "What is it?" He was still up the ladder, looking down at her. Felicity looked up saying:

"Please come down and I will explain." Simon descended from the ladder and leant against it as he waited for her to speak. Why did this woman always make him feel so defenceless? He was thinking this as Felicity tried to get her thoughts under control. If she didn't speak soon, he would just grab her and kiss her, he could see her trembling and he could feel his own body responding.

Felicity suddenly started to speak and the moment was gone. Simon shook himself and concentrated on what she was saying. Ten minutes later, he had agreed to meet her at the studio the next day and as he smiled at her and climbed back up the ladder, she realised her legs were shaking. She went back to her car, rested her head against the steering wheel and thought how his eyes had glittered with those amazing silver specks. She also felt strangely disappointed that he hadn't kissed her; she had so wanted him to. Abruptly, she sat up straight and ground the gears as she drove off, forcing her thoughts away from the thought of Simon's mouth on hers. She drove back to the pub, still trembling and told Lucy and Michael that Simon was going to do the work at the studio. Surprised at this announcement, they exchanged a look which Felicity missed. It spoke volumes between them as they had both noticed her slightly disturbed state when she had walked in. Trouble ahead they both thought.

Simon started work on the studio a couple of days later, he'd been given plans to work to, sketches really but enough for him to know what Felicity wanted. He would be finished in a week had told her, but please keep away as he didn't appreciate people looking over his shoulder. They either trusted him to do the job or not. Rattled, but acceding to his request, Felicity left him alone and concentrated on supplies for the studio and the progress at the cottage. It was slow but steady; all the rooms had been completely gutted. The only things that Felicity wanted kept had been the Aga in the kitchen, the fireplace in the large sitting room and the one in the smallest of the bedrooms. Everything else was being replaced. New flagstones had been laid in the kitchen and hallway and a new staircase was installed. The other floors had been repaired and sanded down ready for carpets. New windows and doors were being fitted, designed to look exactly like the originals, but double-glazed. It was costing her a lot of money, but money she had and she wanted her cottage to be perfect. She was very pleased with the progress.

The one big headache for her was the garden. Between them they had not been able to find anyone to take on this mammoth task. Abe too had tried to locate a gardener through his local contacts but to no avail. Undaunted, Felicity was determined to get the garden back to some semblance of order. She asked Abe if he had anything she could use to start to clear the garden. He searched amongst his tools and found a machete. He used it from time to time when he needed to remove thick undergrowth impeding drainage channels. He showed Felicity how to use it, handed it to her and went back to his work. After a few awkward swings, she got the hang of it and set to work. She decided to tackle the large area which was covered with brambles, nettles and creeping plants that had entwined themselves across the garden. Half an hour later, having cleared a small area and feeling pleased with her progress, she swung the machete once more and it struck something solid amongst the greenery. Her arm shook with the impact, causing her to drop the machete. It hit her foot hard and blood spread rapidly across her shoe. Shocked and horrified she opened her mouth to shout, but fell to the ground, unconscious and bleeding profusely from the deep cut in her foot. As she came to, she heard her name being called,

"I'm in the brambles!" she shouted as loud as she could and as Simon appeared she fainted again with shock and surprise.

Ten

Minutes later, Felicity came to and found herself wrapped in a blanket and a makeshift bandage on her foot. Simon was driving her car too fast, his face grim and set. He had searched her jacket pockets and found the car keys. He wasn't going to wait till she regained consciousness to ask her where they were. She needed urgent attention.

"Where are we going?" she asked, her voice husky and quiet, so quiet she didn't think Simon had heard her.

"What the hell did you think you were doing? You shouldn't have tried to clear that mess. A machete is lethal, those guys shouldn't have given it to you. You could have bled to death. What idiotic notion made you do it?" He thumped his fist on the steering wheel, he was so angry. She wanted to cry, she was cold and shivery and he was shouting at her. She sniffed and he turned to look at her, his eyes dark grey and steely.

"Where are we going?" she asked again, her voice shaking. He glanced at her again and gruffly said:

"The nearest A and E which is in Plymouth." He was starting to shake too; the fact that she could indeed have bled to death affecting him more than he realised. He closed his mind to his train of thought and kept repeating to himself, *She's got my cottage, she's got my cottage*.

Simon screeched to a halt as they arrived at the hospital then picked her up and carried her in. He bypassed Reception and the people patiently waiting to be seen, ignoring the clerk who tried to stop him. He strode up to the nurses' station and demanded that she be seen by a doctor immediately.

"This woman has a deep cut from a machete, she could bleed to death. God knows what germs she has in the wound. She was in deeply covered ground which had a mess and tangle of brambles, nettles and who knows what else. She needs a tetanus shot and probably antibiotics and she's in shock." He stopped to draw breath as a doctor approached.

"Are you her husband?" he asked Simon.

"Good God no," he replied and almost dropped her.

"Bring her in here and wait outside." Simon put her down none too gently on the bed, and marched out oblivious to the stares and astonished looks on the faces of everyone in the department. Felicity's last thought before losing consciousness again was that he had let her go when she had felt so safe in his arms.

She woke to hear a heated argument going on outside the cubicle. She heard Simon's raised voice angrily insisting that he was taking her home right now. No reason the doctor could give would make him change his mind and leave her in the hospital. He couldn't bear the thought of leaving her there alone. She needed to be with the people she knew. Lucy and Michael would take care of her. He marched to the cubicle, swept her up in his arms from the bed and stormed out of the hospital. He dumped her on the back seat, covered her with his jacket and set off back to Little Trenchard.

No words were exchanged, but every so often he thumped the steering wheel muttering "Damn, damn, damn."

He stopped outside the pub, lifted Felicity out of the car, marched inside and with her still in his arms, barked at Lucy:

"Which is her room?" Lucy, for once speechless, pointed up the stairs. He strode off with Lucy close behind. Ray jumped up from his seat and followed. He had eaten dinner at the pub and was having coffee when Simon had burst in. Simon dumped Felicity on the bed, turned to them, took a deep breath and ground out between clenched teeth:

"She could have died, I blame you for this, all of you. Don't let her up for three days and keep her out of that damned garden!"

He stormed off, slammed the door, marched out of the pub slamming that door behind him too. He got back into Felicity's car, drove off like a maniac, parked outside the cottage and shook violently. A few minutes later he got out, locked her car and stood looking at the cottage, his cottage. His mind in a whirl, he walked down the garden and followed the trail Felicity had made with the machete. He soon saw the reason for her accident and his heart skipped a beat. Was this it? Was this what he had been searching for all this time? He looked round him, it was getting dark and he could do nothing tonight, but he knew what he would do tomorrow.

Back at the pub, Lucy fussed round Felicity and when she was settled comfortably, she went down to join Ray and Michael. Ray had related the tale to Michael and when Lucy sat down with them, their main topic of conversation was Simon's behaviour. They had never seen him so incensed, so angry or upset. He had been visibly shaking and the dark steely look in his eyes had darkened when he accused them of being responsible for her accident. Lucy had bridled at this, but Ray calmed her down. He suspected that Simon had accused them through sheer worry for Felicity. Their main priority was to ensure she got better and quickly. She needed to be in the cottage as soon as possible. They had known of Simon's deep interest in the cottage and they were worried he would try to get it away from Felicity. But why? That puzzled them. Why was he so intent on getting the cottage? They would have to keep an eye on him.

Ray decided that he would use his contacts through the business to research the history of the cottage. Maybe that would reveal the interest Simon had. Although Simon had been in the village for a few years, no-one knew much about him. He was popular even though he was short-tempered and very direct. People trusted him and he was honest, but his background was a mystery.

Ray resolved to try to find out who he really was and where he came from. That could solve the mystery of his almost obsessive interest in the cottage.

Eleven

Simon worked through the night and the whole of the next day until very late to complete the workshop. Tired, exhausted from his marathon of re-fitting and decorating, he slept for a few hours, got up and made his way to the cottage. When Abe, Stan and Dave arrived, they were surprised to see Simon hard at work in the garden. Before he could be questioned too much he boldly stated that he was clearing the garden for Felicity as she was incapacitated. They had heard of her accident, nodded to each other and left Simon to his work.

It took him all day to clear the entangled greenery from around the stone obstacle that Felicity had literally bumped into. It was a small structure, not much bigger than a gatepost, but Simon was sure it had some significance, otherwise what was the reason for it being there? He examined it closely. It was solid and had no markings on it so he decided to dig it up, reasoning that it was there as a marker for something. The old lady who had lived here was known to be eccentric.

Next day, Simon was busy digging again, this time with the aid of a mini-digger. Abe and his two young men watched for a while as Simon manipulated the digger, then scratched their heads, shrugged their shoulders and went on with their own work. If that was what Miss Felicity wanted, then so be it. They in turn had decided that she needed a pleasant surprise so they had agreed between them to work late all that week and through the weekend to finish the lower floor. They set to work with a happy will and left Simon to his own devices.

Later that evening Simon had succeeded in completely clearing the overgrown garden back to the line of trees that bordered it. He had discovered a small pond, the remains of a summerhouse and a small orchard. Intrigued now, he cleared the pond, removed the remains of the summerhouse, then pruned and coppiced the small orchard. He would get some fish for the pond and rebuild the summerhouse. All that now remained was for him to dig up the stone post. He was alone now, the workmen had gone for the day and he still had the digger. An hour later, the post was out and there was a hole about five feet deep and two feet wide where the post had been. Simon fixed some ropes to the digger, tied them round his waist and climbed down into the hole armed with a small spade and started to dig around to see if anything was buried there.

It didn't take long before he struck something metallic, unearthing a small metal box about the size of a biscuit tin. It was heavy, well constructed and locked solid. Excited at his find, he knew he must fill in the hole before he tried to open the tin. It was getting dark and he needed to finish here before the light went completely. He hauled himself out of the hole, untied the ropes from the digger, started it up, filled in the hole and levelled the area. It was really dark just as he finished and he didn't see the figure standing amongst the orchard trees. Ray had done his research and now knew what it was that Simon had been searching for; also just why Simon had been so insistent that the cottage was his. He knew Simon was clearing the garden and had gone to the cottage to see exactly what he was doing. He'd seen Simon holding the metal box as he had climbed out of the hole and deduced that he'd found it hidden there. Ray's heart was heavy for Felicity, but he was determined to find out if his own discoveries were in fact proof of what Simon had just unearthed.

Abe had also seen Simon searching where the post had been; he'd returned to the cottage to check the measurements for carpets, wanting to be sure they were correct before placing the order. He too, was intrigued by Simon's actions but kept his own counsel. He would talk to Jeannie later, she was a good listener and usually could work things out.

He left shortly after Simon had gone and related the tale to his lovely young wife. She smiled at Abe as she listened to him, nestled in the crook of his arm as they sat closely together on the sofa. She didn't have an answer for him, but said she would go to see Felicity at the pub. She would probably appreciate a visitor as she must be getting bored being in her room all day. They had met a few times in the village and had liked each other instantly, being of similar ages and as it turned out, of similar interests. Jeannie was a needlewoman, creating patchwork items and enjoying the finer arts of tapestry, cross stitch and knitting. She had an idea of her own forming in her mind and perhaps this could be the right moment to see Felicity and suggest it to her.

Simon went home with his find. Ray returned to his office to continue his research, Abe and Jeannie went upstairs to their room where they happily took great pleasure in ending the day by making love as though they were newlyweds. Felicity, meanwhile, lay wide awake in her bed, not able to get the thought of Simon from her mind. The image of his dark and angry eyes bored into her soul, stopping her from sleeping.

Twelve

Jeannie arrived at the pub with her two children and asked Lucy if she could pop up to see Felicity. Lucy smilingly waved her up the stairs, taking young Bella and her baby brother Sebastian into the kitchen for milk and biscuits. Overjoyed to have a visitor, Felicity immediately asked Jeannie if she could help her get dressed. She was getting up today and venturing downstairs, fed up with being in bed and confined to her room. While she was assisting Felicity, Jeannie told her about the idea she had of helping with the workshops at the studio, shyly telling her about her own hobbies. Perhaps they could run workshops together, combining their skills and interests? Felicity hugged Jeannie, exclaiming that it was an excellent idea, and that as soon as the workshop was finished, Jeannie must visit and they would plan the workshops together.

They chatted and laughed at the antics Felicity went through to get dressed, and then she decided the effort had been too much and she would stay upstairs. Jeannie went down and collected her youngsters and Lucy then decided they would all lunch together in Felicity's room. It turned out to be quite a party, Bella and Sebastian laughed and played, thoroughly enjoying their 'carpet picnic', and the three women had a great time just chatting, especially as Lucy had brought up a bottle of wine which they drank between them.

It was inevitable at some stage that Simon would be mentioned. Felicity casually asked Lucy if she had seen him since he had brought her back to the pub. No, Lucy said, she hadn't seen him at all. She forbore to tell Felicity that he had been working on her garden or the fact that Ray had been researching into his background. Felicity's smile faded and she looked forlorn, her hand unsteady as she lifted her glass to take a drink.

Jeannie had heard from Abe that Felicity and Simon were obviously attracted to each other, but she had not seen for herself how much it affected Felicity. She was surprised how much just the mention of his name unsettled her; he really had got under her skin. She immediately said into the silence following Felicity's question that perhaps they should make a few interim plans for some workshops, before Felicity advertised them. Lucy looked gratefully at Jeannie and agreed it was a great idea. She would be the first on the list to attend, and she could put advertisements in each of the letting rooms, as well as the bar and restaurant. Suddenly the mood in the room changed and Felicity joined in with the planning for the workshops.

An hour later, Jeannie left with a huge smile on her

face, thrilled that she had an outside interest where she could utilise her own skills and hobbies. It would be good fun and give her some independence. She loved Abe dearly, he and the children were her life, but she wanted to keep alive the love they had. She wanted to remain interesting and not drift into boredom and monotony. Maybe even another baby, she thought. Life was so good. She walked gaily back to their own cottage, happy she had lots to tell Abe when he came home. The children were smiling too, even they had caught the air of excitement. When they got home, she would search out all her patterns and templates and the items she had stored away; the products of previous projects she had completed.

She would also ask Abe how Simon was, as she knew he was at the cottage clearing the garden, and now she had witnessed for herself Felicity's reaction to Simon, she wanted to know the whole situation. She was fond of Felicity; they were becoming good friends and she didn't want to see her hurt. Jeannie had agonised for weeks after she had met Abe, willing him to ask her to marry him. He had been so concerned about their age difference, but she had known from the moment he had picked her up off the ground when he knocked her over that he was the right man for her. She had literally fallen for him at that moment. She would have been devastated if Abe had left her, and she could not imagine life without him. She smiled, her nerve ends tingling as she thought about him and the love they shared. She hoped with all her heart that Felicity and Simon could be together.

Thirteen

It was a week since Felicity had injured her foot, and she was dressed and waiting for Michael who was going to drive her to the hospital to have her stitches removed. He knocked on her door and when he saw she was ready, he helped her off the chair and stood by as she manoeuvred her way down the stairs with her crutches, laughing at her wobbly progress. He was going to take her to see the workshop after she'd had her stitches out. Simon had now finished it, not that Felicity knew, and they thought it would be a lovely surprise for her. As they drove along Michael quietly asked her if she had settled down in Little Trenchard; would she ever go back to London? Felicity smiled at the question. She was happy and comfortable; these last few months had given her a sense of peace and security, the dark days had gone and now she could relax and live her life her way. She looked at Michael and found herself telling him about her marriage.

She had been twenty-one when she first met Gordon

James. She had bumped into him as she rushed down the steps from the college. Her books and papers had gone flying and they landed in a heap together on the ground. His briefcase had flown out of his hand and landed on top of her scattered papers. She had started to laugh but stopped immediately when he abruptly pushed her away, picked up his briefcase and stalked off without saying a word. Angry that he hadn't helped her at all, and thinking what a rude man he was, she grabbed her papers and books, rushed after him and demanded to know why he was being so rude. He looked down at her, studying her at length until she began to feel uncomfortable. At last he spoke:

"I am due in Court, you have delayed me and I have no time to waste picking up strangers who do not seem to have the ability to look where they are going. Good day." Astounded and speechless at his curt response, she had dismissed the matter to the back of her mind and gone home.

She related the incident to her mother who was outraged at the rudeness of this man, until that is, she found out who he was. His name had been emblazoned on his briefcase in gold letters and Felicity had subconsciously registered it.

"Gordon James?" her mother had exclaimed, her voice rising to a high pitch. "Don't you know who he is? He is the most brilliant young lawyer in London! He has the most marvellous manner in Court. He is tipped to become a future High Court Judge!" She went off in a rush and a few moments later, Felicity heard her gushing on the phone, apologising profusely for her daughter's behaviour, cajoling as she arranged for a meeting between her daughter and Gordon James so that Felicity could apologise in person for inconveniencing him. She was not the type of woman to be swayed from her views or purpose. She spent her time following the lives of prominent people in the City and Court circles. She made sure she knew who it was best to know and who to avoid in her lifelong quest to become someone of import.

Dumbfounded, Felicity could only stand and listen to her mother; she knew from experience that to say nothing and just acquiesce was the easiest thing to do. Her father had known the same. He had died when she was sixteen and she still missed him. He had driven off to work one morning and had not come home. His car had later been found at the bottom of a steep hill, deep in the bushes where it had obviously crashed. The coroner's verdict had been accidental death, but Felicity was convinced he had driven off the edge deliberately. His wife was too cruel, she had made his life a complete misery and enough was enough. It was hard for a sixteen year old to understand, but her mother would not talk about the death of her husband, so Felicity grieved alone.

The meeting between Gordon and Felicity had been awkward, but at the end of the arranged lunch, he asked her out so she agreed to please her mother, she could not bear to think of the recriminations if she had refused. Her mother encouraged this further meeting, persuading Felicity that he was a good catch and she would not find anyone better as a future husband even though he was ten years older. Horrified at the way her mother was thinking, Felicity realised she had been cleverly manipulated into this relationship. Gordon and her mother immediately recognised in each other a ruthless ambitious streak to pursue and get what they wanted no matter what; they were kindred spirits.

Before she realised what was happening, she was engaged to Gordon, the marriage was announced and then she was in the Registry Office with just a few people, most of whom she didn't know and thirty minutes later, she was Mrs Huntley-James. Gordon and her mother had agreed between them that a double barrelled name sounded so much grander than just plain James. They had a short honeymoon in Paris. Gordon had been a rough and unsympathetic lover caring only for his own needs. Felicity had cried on their wedding night, mostly because the experience had left her feeling bereft and unfulfilled. That never changed and she became fearful of making love, fully aware that Gordon was angry at her lack of response. Just once she had tried to tell him she needed gentleness and tenderness from him. She had cringed when he turned on her, snarling at her that it was her duty to please him and not to demand what she wanted!

They moved into the townhouse and Gordon had taken all her familiar old clothes from her, packed them into black bags and told her to put them in the charity shop. With her mother in tow, he had marched her off to the West End and bought what they considered to be suitable for the lifestyle they would be leading as he was an up and coming barrister. Her mother was in her element and encouraged Gordon's treatment of her daughter. He revelled in the hero worship he received from his mother-in-law and between them they manipulated Felicity into the mould of the wife they considered she should be.

Several attempts by Felicity to find a teaching job, which she had trained for, were immediately dismissed as being most unsuitable for her position in life. She should concentrate on being the perfect hostess that Gordon Huntley-James needed in his quest for recognition as a leading light in Law. He rarely spent time with her, immediately shutting himself in his study each night as soon as dinner was over. She was never allowed in that room, he had expressly forbidden her to enter, it was his private space and nothing to do with her. He had employed a cleaner, she tidied his room, therefore Felicity had no need to go in there.

He became more and more angry as time went on that she hadn't conceived. He could not understand it, he wanted an heir, it would be good for his image and the townhouse was big enough to accommodate a nanny. Felicity had, many months previously, made the decision that on no account would she give this man a child. She knew what would happen, the baby would be taken from her and would be brought up in the manner Gordon considered 'suitable'. It horrified her that she might conceive a child with this man, so she made sure she could not become pregnant. It wasn't that she didn't want children, just not with this man. They had been married for nearly two years when one morning before he left for work, Gordon had shouted at Felicity, demanding that she see a specialist as there must be something wrong with her, she should have been pregnant long ago. He had arranged a clinic appointment for her and insisted she attend to find out why she hadn't conceived. His love-making had become more brutal and he frightened her. Before she could stop herself she had yelled back at him that there was nothing wrong with her, she had just made sure she would not get pregnant, she didn't want him as the father of her children.

His face drained of all colour, he snarled at her, he was angrier than she had ever seen him and she realised she had gone too far. He picked up the telephone, spoke briefly to his secretary saying he was delayed. He crashed the phone back on its receiver, grabbed Felicity and dragged her to the bedroom. He threw her on the bed and raped her, not once but twice. He beat her into submission, bruising her face and subsequently her body. He got up and searched the drawers and cupboards until he found her pills. He took these with him and his parting words were that she would give in to his demands until she became pregnant and he would make damn sure she did. He stormed out of the house and she heard his sports car revving up as he drove off in anger.

She never knew why she went to the window, but she watched as his car sped up the hill and went through the red lights. He hit the lorry head on. His car flipped up and somersaulted over the cab of the lorry then crashed down onto the road, landing upside down, a mangled wreck. She had fainted, waking to find two policemen in the bedroom gently picking her up and trying to be kind in telling her that her husband had died instantly in a car crash. Her immediate thought was relief that she was free of this man, then contrition at that thought, then horror at what she knew her mother would say. The policemen had noticed the bruises on her face and when they questioned her about it, she said it must have happened when she fainted. They accepted this even though through experience they doubted it was the truth.

The next few weeks were a whirl of questions and answers: the inquest, the funeral, the journalists and newspaper reports. Worst of all was her mother. She had ranted and raved at Felicity, telling her over and over that she had caused the accident, it was her fault entirely. If she had done as Gordon wanted and given him an heir, it would not have happened. Even when Felicity told her mother about Gordon raping her, it made no difference, the only response she got was that she had deserved it. Months of this constant haranguing from her mother took its toll. Felicity needed tranquillisers and sleeping pills to stop herself from thinking about the accident which by this time she believed she had caused.

Michael had listened in silence, his emotions as she told her story running through surprise, horror, anger and complete sympathy. He turned to look at her and saw she was smiling, he smiled in returned and guessed she would never leave Little Trenchard. She was obviously happy now and something within her had changed, she was alight with life. He couldn't believe that she had come through such a dreadful and shocking experience and be smiling so happily. He felt privileged that she had related her story to him; he would not repeat it to anyone, it was for her to tell if she wanted to.

Felicity knew she was in Little Trenchard to stay, she was meant to be here and Simon was here too. She sighed softly and smiled as she thought about him, her whole body alive and tingling.

Fourteen

Felicity's eyes lit up when she saw her workshop. Simon had excelled himself, it looked even better than she had imagined. It was light and airy, compact but not crowded. The storage was hidden under the worktops, the shelving above was adjustable; it was just perfect. The tables she had purchased could be moved around as necessary, she could buy more if required, there was plenty of room. It was magnificent, she could start work immediately on her own projects and she could now advertise the workshop sessions that she and Jeannie had planned.

She was so excited she hugged Michael, her eyes shining and her obvious enthusiasm made him want to jump with joy. He grabbed her hand and said:

"Come on Felicity, we must tell the others." They went to the car smiling and laughing. Lucy was thrilled for Felicity when she heard about the workshop, declared she was eager to assist and she would be the first one in the door at the initial session. The excitement was infectious and seemed to fill the whole place, everyone was smiling and laughing, it was almost as though they were holding a party. Lucy spotted Ray at the door, he was beckoning her over and she frowned, puzzled that he didn't just come in. She knew her brother very well and was aware he had a special feeling for Felicity. She was worried too as Ray had been somewhat preoccupied for the last few days; she would question him about it to find out what was wrong. Excusing herself she left the bar and went over to him. He said nothing but walked into the pub garden obviously expecting her to follow him. He sat down and briefly explained, he knew he could trust Lucy to say nothing, so he told her of his discovery.

The old lady who had owned the cottage had been known locally as Grace but it appeared that wasn't her first name, she had been christened Isobel Grace. She had never married, kept herself to herself and was somewhat of an eccentric. She became very reclusive. The cottage, (never known as anything other than 'The Cottage'), gradually became more and more decrepit as she would not allow anyone to repair it. Finally, she lived in the kitchen, going upstairs only to use the bathroom. When she had died, the deeds to the property had been found in a box, along with her birth certificate. Two letters were also in the box, both from a man named Christopher Mason, the address on them from a town in Northern Scotland. The information in the letters showed he was her nephew and a simple line written by Grace on the bottom of one of these letters stated that he was to inherit the cottage.

Ray stopped for a moment and Lucy waited for him to continue, she didn't want to distract him by asking the many questions that had sprung to her mind. He continued by saying that when Felicity had asked him to complete her purchase of the cottage, he had simply put the papers together in legal form and they were signed and witnessed accordingly. The money was handed over to Mr Mason with his set of the legal documents and that was that. He had decided when it became apparent that Simon was desperate to get the cottage that he would dig into the background of the old lady. He searched local parish and council papers, made extensive enquires through the Land Registry Office and went to St Catherine's House (where a copy of all births, deaths and marriages are kept) to research Grace's family tree. All he had was the birth certificate but he persevered.

He discovered that Grace had worked as a housemaid in London for a very well known family with many properties in that city. She was fifteen when the owner of the house had taken a liking to her and pursued her one night, his intention being to take this young woman to his bed. She was raped by this man, beaten until she was unable to resist. The result being that when she appeared bruised and with black eyes the next morning she was immediately dismissed from the household. Two months later, she discovered she was pregnant.

She ended up in a hostel and when she gave birth to her child, a girl, the baby immediately went for adoption by another wealthy family in London whose business was a very successful Law Office. She was educated well, became a lady and married a lawyer named Geoffrey Gordon James. Lucy's eyes opened wide, Gordon James had been the name of Felicity's late husband! Surely this couldn't be the same family. The couple had one child, a son who they named Simon, but the mother died in childbirth and Geoffrey James never acknowledged his son as he blamed him for the death of his wife. He re-married two years later and they also had a son, named Gordon, the same Gordon James who Felicity had married. He had been spoilt, educated at the best private schools and followed his father into the family business. He was a ruthless and selfish man, used to getting his own way and oblivious of other people's needs and wants.

Ray paused and briefly explained to Lucy how he had found out all this information. It transpired that the hostel, still in existence, had kept a journal written by Grace, detailing the events of her life. They also had the details of the adoption and Ray had pursued this line of enquiry. It had been quite simple for him to follow the story as the family was so well known in the circles of law. He drew a deep breath and continued his tale.

Simon, meanwhile, neglected by his father and step-mother, had virtually been raised by a local farmer and his wife. They had befriended Simon when he turned up at their farm one day with a broken arm having fallen from one of their trees whilst scrumping apples. The farm had been situated on the edge of one of the parks near London, and was in easy reach of the suburb where the

James family lived. The old farmer, still alive, had been happy to chat about the boy Simon. They had liked him and had kept in contact, albeit infrequently. They had given Ray quite an insight to Simon's character.

As soon as he could, Simon left London, travelling around the country doing odd jobs and picking up skills along the way. This was how he'd learnt his woodwork and carpentry skills. He'd learnt something of his family background from gossip and searching family papers kept in the library. He'd found a piece of card used as a bookmark which depicted a picture of a small village in Devon. The name Grace had been scrawled on the back of the card and instinct made him take this card, sure it must mean something. His grandmother had been called Grace so he decided he would find this place in Devon. It took Simon considerable time to find the village, eventually arriving at Little Trenchard. The scraps of information he gathered fitted together in his mind like a jigsaw and he became certain that more information must be hidden at the cottage. He was sure he was the rightful heir to the property after he had researched his family history in much the same way as Ray had done. On one of his rare visits back to the farm, Simon had told the old farmer what he had discovered about his family.

Lucy sat back, amazed and dismayed at the same time.

"Are you sure?" she asked Ray. He nodded, Simon was half-brother to Felicity's late husband and as a direct blood descendant to Grace, in fact her grandson, then he was almost certainly the rightful heir to the cottage.

"Ray," Lucy blurted out. "Are you in love with Felicity?"

"Yes I am," he replied. "But not in the way you think. Katherine was the love of my life; I still love her now and could never replace her. I love Felicity as the daughter I never had from the first moment I met her and I will defend her and fight for her as any father would."

Lucy's eyes filled with tears of relief and worry. She knew Ray was sincere, it was a real relief to know his love for Felicity was as a father and he wouldn't be hurt. She worried though about the impact Ray's discoveries might have on Felicity. And Simon? What of him and his right to the cottage? They must have a talk with Michael, he'd told Lucy that Felicity had given him an insight into her former life and marriage, that her husband had been cruel and violent to her. What if Simon had inherited the same nature? They knew he could get angry, they had witnessed that for themselves; but violent? Lucy's heart sank, she had sensed the chemistry between Simon and Felicity, she was completely aware of the impact he had on their new friend. She was sure Felicity was in love with Simon, though not aware of it herself as she was in denial as far as men were concerned. Her eyebrows shot up, Simon had been so distressed when Felicity had been injured, so angry yet caring at the same time. *Oh my God,* she thought, what would happen when he found out that she had been married to his half brother?

Fifteen

Unaware of what was happening in the background, Felicity hobbled from the pub to her cottage. The workmen rushed out to greet her and gently guide her into the finished kitchen, proud of their work and so pleased they could surprise her. She couldn't believe her eyes and was so overwhelmed she burst into tears. A grubby handkerchief and garden chair were produced, and a cup of tea poured from a flask into a tin mug was pressed into her hands. The three workmen were gathered round her, not sure what to say or do. She gulped the tea and then smiled through her tears.

"Thank you all so much, it's beautiful," she said and held out her hands to them. They hugged her in turn and all started to talk at once, now guiding her through the rest of the rooms. She couldn't believe how wonderful it looked, the character had been retained, but it was all new and looked incredible. Not long now she was told, by the middle of November they would be finished. Just a few more weeks and she could move in. Abe suggested that she think about the furniture to ensure it could be delivered when the work was finished. Felicity wandered about as the workmen went back to their tasks upstairs. Eventually she went out into the garden; she knew it had been cleared. Smatterings of conversation had come to her ears and she was sure she had heard Simon's name mentioned, but dismissed it as he had been working on her workshop.

She was amazed at the difference; she could now see the whole shape of the garden and how it flowed right round the cottage. She noticed the small orchard and was delighted, there was a pond too! She went closer and noticed the fish swimming round. Where had they come from? She saw the concrete base that looked as though it must have had a building of some sort on it at some time. The mature trees had been cut back and all the creeping greenery, brambles and nettles had disappeared. She could do so much with this garden, maybe have some chickens, grow vegetables and lots of herbs; the space at the back of the kitchen would be ideal for a herb garden.

She walked round to the other side of the cottage, here she could plant a flower garden, all those varieties that she loved which she could paint watercolours of and also dry them for her collages.

Lost in her thoughts she didn't hear the van arrive. It wasn't until she limped back round to the kitchen that she saw the pile of wood and glass laid out on the ground. Simon came through the gate carrying a saw and tool bag. He stopped dead when he saw her and for a few moments they stood immobilized just looking at each other.

"What are you doing?" Felicity asked him.

"Working, what does it look like?" he gruffly replied. He turned away, then stopped and looked back at her. "I'm replacing the summerhouse that used to be here," he said more gently.

"But why?" she asked.

"Because I want to," was the reply, "I want the cottage to look right and the summerhouse is part of that!"

Stung by this remark she blurted out:

"It's my cottage, not yours and I wish you would keep out."

Tears sprung in her eyes and she hobbled off as quick as she could, out of the gate and back along the road. She sat down in the pub garden, her shoulders heaving as she sobbed, the anguish, hurt and distress finally released. It only seemed seconds later when she found herself being cradled and hugged in strong arms and a soothing voice saying:

"Don't cry my darling, don't cry, please don't cry. I can't bear to see you so unhappy."

Next thing she knew, her face was being turned up to his, then his mouth kissing her fiercely and hungrily. She melted into him, her lips and body responding to his ardency, her eyes tightly shut. Abruptly, he let her go, she fell back onto the seat, bereft and alone, her mouth throbbing, her legs trembling.

Lucy had seen the whole incident, she had been about to go out into the garden when she caught sight of Felicity in such distress and crying so hard. She'd just stepped out of the pub when Simon had rushed through the gate. *Oh my God*, she had thought for the second time that day. Her next thought as she approached Felicity, after Simon had rushed off, was that the path of true love never ran smooth.

Simon walked and walked after he had left Felicity so suddenly. He walked away from the village, his heart thumping in his chest, his breathing erratic and every nerve end in his body tingling, he was shaking uncontrollably. He couldn't get the feel and touch of Felicity out of his mind, she had set his whole body alight with desire for her. He groaned and leant against a tree, his legs would not carry him any further. He slid to the ground and rested his back against the tree.

Damn that woman, why did she have to come to this village? He'd been out with women before, had a couple of relationships that lasted for a while, had made love to those women, but never before had anyone made him feel as he did for Felicity. She had burrowed into his inner soul and just to look at her set his senses alight. He trembled when he was near her and the feel of her in his arms, the touch of her and the response he'd felt when he kissed her had lit a flame within him. It was smouldering deep inside him. He'd left her so suddenly before he made a complete fool of himself and declared his love for her. Love? He sat bolt upright. Love? What on earth was he thinking? He couldn't possibly be in love with her, he hardly knew her. That fact though was of no consequence, he was in love. He groaned again and stood up, he had no idea exactly where he was but he must make his way back to the village, he had to erect the summerhouse. He set off, back in the direction he had come from, his mind whirling round with just one thought – the feel of Felicity in his arms, her body melting into his.

Sixteen

Several things happened during that afternoon, Simon hammered and sawed and worked as though possessed, building the summerhouse. The three workmen dared not approach him, his expression was unfathomable; best leave him alone.

Lucy cornered Michael and demanded he tell her the circumstances of Felicity's life before she came to the village. After relating to him the incident she had witnessed, he swore her to secrecy and told her. She too went through similar emotions Michael had on hearing Felicity's story, horrified that she had been raped by her own husband. Calming herself from the anger she felt on Felicity's behalf, she told Michael about the information Ray had discovered.

Ray went to see a close friend of his, a respected solicitor and asked him to clarify if Simon had a real and sure claim on the cottage.

Felicity closed her mind on Simon's kiss and her own response which had shaken her to the core. She could still feel his mouth on hers, she couldn't stop trembling and her whole body was craving his touch. She threw herself into moving her art equipment to the workshop in preparation to begin her small business. Once done, she stood at her easel, picked up her brushes and painted as though her life depended on it.

After two hours of frenzied painting, she stood back to survey her work. She drew her breath in sharply and tears welled in her eyes. Simon was looking back at her from the painting. His eyes were on fire, smoky grey with beautiful silver glints alight with desire, his mouth was just starting to smile. She had painted him perfectly and she knew it was the best work she had ever done. Her fingers went to her mouth, remembering the feel of his lips on hers and how she had responded. She groaned from deep within herself, her legs buckled and she fell to the floor, once more sobbing uncontrollably.

The last thing to happen on this eventful day was a new visitor to the pub. A very well dressed woman got out of a taxi and walked in followed by the bemused driver carrying her luggage. She curtly told him to leave it by the bar, paid him the fare then turned to Lucy and said:

"I believe my daughter Mrs Huntley-James is staying here."

Seventeen

Lucy immediately guessed who this woman was and not being easily brow-beaten, she replied honestly:

"No-one of that name is staying here. Can I get you something?"

Felicity's mother was not used to anyone being forthright with her so she was somewhat flustered at the reply. Gathering herself together she asked if a room was available for the night and she would like tea. Lucy forbore to reply until she had checked the accommodation book, taking her time even though she knew rooms were available. She was biding her time trying to work out how she could warn Felicity.

"A single room is available on the second floor, it is £35 for bed and breakfast, all our rooms are en-suite. Would that be convenient for you? Would you like your tea here or in your room?"

Michael was listening from behind the kitchen door, and couldn't believe his ears. Tea in the room? They never did that! Knowing his wife so well he knew there must be a good reason for her suggestion, he waited and listened.

"Yes, that will be fine, I will go straight up, you may bring the tea to me there, plain biscuits with the tea, nothing fancy."

Lucy put on her best face, smiling through clenched teeth at the rudeness of this dreadful woman.

"Excuse me for a moment, I will just get my husband to take your luggage up." She went quickly into the kitchen, gave Michael the key, told him it was Felicity's mother, to say nothing about Felicity staying there, and as soon as she had arranged the tea she would be off to find her. Michael, now in a whirl, also put on his best face, carried the luggage up and dashed back to the kitchen. Lucy gave him the tray, tea for one with two very plain biscuits, not her usual plateful of fancy bits and pieces. He chuckled as he realised the reason for the sparseness of the plate knowing that he would place a bet on his wife winning this particular battle of wills!

Lucy called Felicity on her mobile asking where she was, then quickly made her way there in the pub van. As she drove along, she worried about what state Felicity was in. She was obviously upset. Lucy had heard it in her voice when she had answered the phone. What had happened?

When she arrived at the workshop, she found Felicity very distressed, still crying and covering the easel with a large white sheet. Horrified that she was still so tormented, Lucy couldn't decide how to break the news about her mother turning up at the pub. Felicity turned away from the easel and threw herself into Lucy's arms, sobbing on her shoulder and muttering "Simon, oh Simon," as she cried herself out.

Lucy said nothing, just held her until she quietened down and stopped crying. Before Felicity could ask anything, Lucy told her that Mrs Huntley was in the pub and she was staying the night in room 12. Felicity managed a weak smile. Room 12 was the furthest room from the bar, also the smallest, always the last room to be let out. It was clean and comfortable, just not the best room. She saw the funny side of this and had a new respect for Lucy and her judgement.

"She asked if her daughter Mrs Huntley-James was staying in the pub, so I told her no-one of that name was staying there," Lucy said. This was true of course but Felicity's mother would not appreciate the play on words. Felicity smiled again and Lucy suggested she rinsed her face and they would go back together to face the dragon. Felicity laughed out loud at this so apt description of her mother and like two giggling schoolgirls, they returned to the pub.

On the way back, Felicity confessed to Lucy that she hadn't contacted her mother since leaving London. Lucy made no comment, just raised her eyebrows. Having heard about the treatment Felicity had received from her mother, she could well understand why she didn't wish to contact her.

Mrs Huntley was sitting in the bar, drumming her fingers on the table impatiently when Lucy walked in with Felicity.

"Lissy, where have you been?" she demanded of her daughter. "This woman told me you weren't here!" She waved dismissively at Lucy as she made this statement.

Lucy completely ignored the woman and went to the kitchen to find Michael, her hackles well and truly raised. Felicity sat across from her mother, said nothing and waited for the tirade to begin.

"I cannot believe you want to stay here in this back of beyond place. You didn't contact me as you said you would. I have spent weeks searching for you. You should be in London with me, you should never have sold the townhouse. Your mother-in-law is devastated that you have deserted us. Your place is with your family, we could have grieved together. And living in a pub! What would Gordon have thought! He was so good to you and this is how you repay him. You are a disgrace to us all, thoughtless and have no concern for anyone but yourself. Go get your bags packed, I have ordered a taxi for nine thirty tomorrow morning to take us back to London. You will come home with me. Now go and do as I say, I will not take no for an answer."

As she stopped to draw breath, Felicity stood up and looked down at this woman who had given birth to her, who had been so cruelly unsympathetic when she was told Gordon had raped her daughter. How could she have condoned something that dreadful? What sort of woman was she to think her own daughter had deserved such inhuman treatment? Her whole young life had been made a misery by this selfish, cold and unfeeling woman who had not an ounce of warmth or love in her. Felicity could not forgive or forget that she had driven her father to his death and now she had driven Felicity from her. She could no longer bring herself to use the word 'Mother'. She drew a deep breath and said:

"I hope this is the last time I have to speak to you, my life is my own, I will do as I please. You no longer have any control over me. As for Gordon James, the man was cruel and abusive. He was a violent, selfish bully and he raped me twice, hoping he could get me pregnant. I thank the Lord that never happened. I have no wish to be associated with you or any member of his family ever again, as far as I am concerned, you and they can all go to hell."

She turned away and walked out of the bar, away from her mother, shaking at what she had said but now completely, totally free of all that had been bad in her life. Mrs Huntley sagged down in the chair and for the first time in her life felt alone, she had no-one. Lucy and Michael, having listened from the kitchen and knowing the whole story, just looked at each other, dismay and worry on their faces.

Eighteen

An hour later, Mrs Huntley was in a taxi on her way back to London. Felicity was in her room, exhausted, sleeping, but fitfully, her sleep interrupted by visions of Simon, the feel of his mouth on hers and the wonderful sensation of being held close to him. Lucy and Michael had temporarily closed the pub *'due to unforeseen circumstances, open again at 6 pm.'* and had gone to see Ray. He in turn had just returned from his friend's office with news he hadn't wanted to hear.

6 pm saw the bar open again, Lucy, Ray and Michael ensconced in the snug bar while the bar staff coped with the customers. Lucy told Ray about the meeting between Felicity and her mother. Ray smiled in admiration of Felicity at the way she had dismissed her mother. He then drew in his breath as he realised the significance of her last words to that dreadful woman. Lucy and Michael nodded in agreement at Ray's concern. What would happen if and when Felicity found out about Simon's relationship to her late husband? They couldn't come up

with any answers to the problems they saw looming ahead. Why did life have to be so complicated? They decided the best policy was to stay close to Felicity and just watch and wait to see what happened.

Felicity came down to the bar a little later, pale and completely drained. She told her friends she was going for a walk; she needed air and had to think.

She walked aimlessly, not really knowing where she was heading and eventually realised she had wandered on to the moor. It was beginning to get dark and so she turned to make her way back. She could see her cottage in the distance. There was a light inside, but no-one should be there! She quickened her pace and half an hour later she was walking up the path. Carefully she opened the door and went inside.

Everything was quiet, she couldn't hear anything. The light she had seen was still on and was coming from the small room off the kitchen, now turned into the utility room. She crept across the kitchen, the door to the utility room was ajar and Simon was standing looking at papers he had spread on the work surface. They looked old and grubby and were torn. He was frowning as he traced the marks on the papers. From her position, Felicity could just make out that they were plans, but of what? Simon shuffled the papers and uncovered a sheet with spidery writing all over it. He picked it up and read through it then suddenly he exclaimed:

"I knew I was right, I always knew it! It's mine, by right, it *is* mine!"

Felicity's sharp intake of breath registered with

Simon, he turned round quickly and opened the door wide before she could move. She stood motionless, her heart thumping, her legs quivering, her breath caught in her throat. He grabbed hold of her arms and asked if she'd heard what he had just said. She nodded, her eyes drawn to his mouth and then swiftly, before she reached up to put her mouth against his, she raised her eyes to look directly into his.

"So now you know," he said harshly, still holding her arms tightly, his grip tightening, his smoky grey eyes boring deep into her soul.

Nineteen

Felicity couldn't drag her eyes away from his, they were dark and smouldering, but as they stood just staring at each other, his eyes darkened to almost black and the silver glints appeared. She groaned from deep within her, not aware that her own eyes were alight with desire. Simon drew her nearer, his mouth descended on hers and she was lost, her body falling into his as he held her fast, his mouth asking questions which her body unashamedly said yes to.

He scooped her up in his arms and carried her upstairs, he kicked one of the bedroom doors open and laid her gently on the floor, now covered in soft new carpet. He slowly undressed her, caressing her as he did so and she found herself revelling in the feel of his skin as she slowly undressed him, responding to his every touch and move. Tenderly he made love to her, caringly, lovingly, exploring her body, pleasing her with his hands and mouth. For Felicity, the feeling was so intense, so ecstatic, so wonderfully satisfying, she didn't want it to end. She found herself responding to his every touch and she knew that her own caresses of Simon were making him feel as she did. She explored his body the way he did hers. When finally they reached the heights of their love-making she felt as though an eternal fire had been lit inside her, never to go out, to smoulder and then to burst into flames at his touch. Simon held her close, raining small kisses on her face, gently caressing her back and arms, wanting her to know how he felt. How did he feel? Words wouldn't come to him. Never before had a woman made him feel like this, never before had any woman responded to him as Felicity had. Now he really knew what it meant for two people to become as one.

Felicity had fallen asleep in his arms. Simon gently laid her on the carpet and covered her with her dress, then dressed himself and quietly left. He had to think, had to plan. Why? How had he allowed this to happen? His body still quivered, the feel and taste of her still with him. He knew he should stay, he wanted to, but how could he? She didn't know who he really was. He now knew her late husband was his half brother. He had overheard the conversation she'd had with her mother. He'd been about to enter the pub when he'd heard the raised voice of Felicity's mother. The door had been ajar and he'd stopped when he heard Felicity speak. Stunned by what he'd heard, he had turned round and walked away. If she found out his relationship to her late husband, how could she, would she ever let him into her life? Damn, damn, damn, what could he do?

As he left the cottage, Ray saw him go across the

garden. They'd got worried when Felicity hadn't come home and as she hadn't answered their phone calls, they went out looking for her. Ray had gone to the cottage and wondered whether to look inside for her but some instinct kept him from doing so. He called Lucy and Michael and told them he thought he knew where she was and he would see them back at the pub. He left the cottage after he had seen Simon go, he was convinced Felicity was there, equally convinced he knew what had occurred between these two. His not so old heart remembered the exquisite feeling of that wonderful experience; he and his wife had matched each other so well and he missed it. He was sorrowful for them also as knowing their life historys, he couldn't see a happy ending. As soon as Lucy saw Ray's expression she knew, she had known in her heart it was inevitable, but she too was sorrowful for them both. Her own expression as she looked at Michael spoke volumes to him, he too knew how it felt to love well together.

Felicity woke and immediately realised she was alone, Simon had gone! Quickly she dressed and made her way back to the pub, she didn't want to see anyone so she went quietly up the back stairs to her room. She undressed, went into the shower and turned the taps on letting the warm water wash over her body. The soft, sensual caress of the water as it flowed over her made her whole body tingle as she closed her mind to all thoughts except those of Simon and how they had made love. She leant against the wall, lost in her thoughts and feelings, her body still shaking from Simon's touch. The water caressed her skin, wakening her desire for Simon. How she wished he was with her now, how she wished they were standing under the shower together enjoying each other as the water washed softly over them. She opened her eyes abruptly, she must stop these wanton thoughts. Wanton? No, just pure love and deep desire for the man who had buried himself in her heart and soul.

A sudden knock on the door shook her from her thoughts. She quickly turned off the taps as she heard Lucy calling to her, asking if she was ok. Felicity grabbed a towel, wrapped herself in it and went to the door.

"I was in the shower, I am about to go to bed," she replied to Lucy through the closed door, her voice husky as she spoke.

Lucy, smiling at the deep tone of Felicity's voice, just quietly said, "See you in the morning."

Twenty

Next morning Felicity went down to the kitchen, a fire still smouldering in her eyes. Both Lucy and Michael felt the impact of it and for a few moments couldn't speak. Felicity sat down, oblivious of her friend's reaction. Lucy brought her a mug of tea asking if she was ok. She nodded, her mind still on last evening, her body still quivering with delight and desire. Even the touch of her clothes against her skin made her nerve ends tingle. Suddenly, she stood up and asked if Lucy would take her to the workshop as they had left her car there yesterday. Lucy agreed and they were sat quietly in the workshop when her phone rang interrupting their thoughts. It was Michael.

"Keep your expression neutral Lucy, Simon has gone. He gave Ray the keys to his flat earlier this morning and said he would be back sometime. Wouldn't tell Ray where he was going. Stay there with Felicity." He rang off and Lucy stared at the phone. Felicity frowned at her:

"Is everything ok? You've gone quite pale."

Lucy forced a smile and nodded then quickly explained that Justin had finished at uni earlier than he expected and was on his way home. A small lie but it was all she could think of to say on the spur of the moment. She turned away from Felicity and fiddled with the mugs, absentmindedly switched the kettle on and then off again, trying to work out how she could keep Felicity occupied.

"Do you feel like a trip to Plymouth to look for your linen and curtains?" she suddenly asked.

Felicity nodded, she needed a distraction to take her mind off her whirling thoughts and feelings. After a quick call to Michael to let him know what was happening and that they would be back by six, they set off to Plymouth. The next couple of hours were spent buying duvets, bed linen and towels. Curtains she couldn't find so she decided to make her own, it would give her another project to focus on after she had moved in.

Felicity had ordered beds for two of the bedrooms, the third she was turning into a small sitting room for herself; she would hang her painting in there, it would be her own private room and she would have Simon for company. Happy with this thought she smiled, her whole face coming alight. She leant back in the car seat, closed her eyes and let her mind dwell on Simon and their lovemaking. She could feel him, feel his touch and her whole body shuddered from the memory. Lucy sensed she didn't want to talk, she could see her trembling and felt happy for her. Oh how she wished Simon hadn't gone, she would speak to Ray and find out the details.

They arrived back at the pub to find Michael trying to deal with three sets of visitors all wanting rooms. Lucy and Felicity pitched in as a sudden rush of early evening customers wanting drinks and dinner descended on the pub. Michael fled back to his kitchen; he was happy in his own domain and more than happy to leave the logistics to the women. It was after eight o'clock before things had quietened down; Felicity went up to her room, so Lucy took the chance to call Ray.

She kept quiet as he explained to her the events leading to Simon going. He had decided to travel across France and visit some old school friends and didn't know how long he would be away. He'd asked Ray to keep an eye on his rented flat as he would be back at some stage. Ray was the managing agent for the landlord so was well aware that Simon had recently renewed the lease and it had ten months to run. He had insisted vehemently to Simon that he must leave a contact telephone number. Reluctantly Simon had agreed but not before he had extracted a promise from Ray not to reveal it to anyone.

What Ray didn't tell Lucy was that he'd asked Simon directly about his supposed right to the cottage, telling him at the same time he knew the details through his research. Simon had neither confirmed nor denied it, he just cryptically replied that the matter could be decided before he returned, then there would be no problem. Ray had also asked if he would definitely be returning and Simon asked why he wanted to know. Ray replied in his own cryptic way that come Christmas, Simon would be needed back in the village. Understanding was reached between both men without more words being exchanged. They shook hands and Ray smiled as Simon left, certain that before long he would be back.

Twenty-One

Felicity was puzzled. A few weeks had gone by, she'd not heard from Simon and no-one had seen him. No-one knew where he'd gone. She'd asked Lucy, Michael and Ray if they knew, but they all denied any knowledge of his whereabouts. She suspected Ray knew something but he refused to be drawn. He had promised Simon he wouldn't reveal his location even though he was stricken for Felicity. He felt so bad about the knowledge he had and couldn't pass on to Felicity, but Simon had been so insistent he must keep it to himself. She had no contact number for him and after she had driven to his flat a few times, she realised that he really had just disappeared. She was disconsolate, she missed him, desperately wanted to be with him, but she had no means of communication. Her moods swung between being angry and hurt, distressed and despairing. She was convinced her friends knew something and were protecting her. But from what? She felt hurt and betrayed, not only by Simon but by Ray, Lucy and Michael. But she was alone, she needed her friends.

She threw herself into organising the rest of her furniture and arranging delivery ready for when she moved into the cottage and shut her mind to her longing for Simon. She had agreed with Lucy and Michael that she would move out of the pub on the 1 December and move into the cottage, just one week away.

Her foot was fully healed and she had marked out her herb bed, it was beginning to get too cold for digging but at least she could plan. Her furniture arrived and was put in place by the delivery team. Stan and Dave were now painting the outside of the cottage and Abe was finally repairing the rickety gate. The hedge had been cut back and almost everything had been done. Abe asked Felicity what name she would give to the cottage. It should have a name he said, it now deserved something better than just 'The Cottage'. Surprised he had asked her, Abe then explained that he and the boys wanted to make her a name plate, their home coming gift to her. Touched and pleased, she said she would let him know when she had decided on an appropriate name. He went away whistling and smiling happily, she had been such a joy to work for, they had all enjoyed it so much and had taken extra care to make sure everything was just as she wanted.

Felicity wandered upstairs thinking about Abe's offer. She meandered into the small room she was turning into her sitting room. The fireplace she had kept; it was so beautiful she hadn't wanted it removed. She loved this room, it was where Simon had made love to her. She lay down on the carpet reliving the whole wonderful experience and the feelings that haunted her every day. As she lay there, the name for the cottage slipped into her mind. Abruptly she sat up. It had to be that, nothing else would be right. Tomorrow she would tell Abe and then she would go to Plymouth and find some chairs and a small table for her room. She would ask Abe to build her some shelves for the end wall for all her books. Happy with these plans she then decided to bring her painting from the workshop and hang it on the wall above the fireplace for when she moved in, she wanted it here for that day, then Simon would be with her.

She lay down again and closed her eyes, how she missed him, how she loved him. She knew then that her love for him had grown from the moment she first saw him. Where was he? Why didn't he contact her? How could he have left her alone for so long? She was so sure he loved her. No-one, no two people could love the way they had unless they were in love with each other.

Tears welled in her eyes, she felt them run down her face and into the carpet. Suddenly she leapt up and dashed into the bathroom. A few minutes later, shaking and shivery, she sat on the bathroom floor realising instantly why she had been so sick. A smile spread across her face, she yelled aloud with joy, it had to be, it must be! Oh, she did hope so! She didn't care if Simon wasn't here, she had part of him growing inside her. She all but skipped into the pub, hugged Lucy and Michael and went up to her room. Startled, they watched her skip away happily wondering what on earth had happened to make her suddenly so joyful. On the way to her room

Felicity was planning; tomorrow, first thing she would buy a test kit just to confirm her thoughts, but she knew in her heart she was right.

Ray; she would go to see Ray. He must know where Simon was. She rushed back downstairs to see Ray coming in the door. Quickly she went across to him, Ray had never seen her so vivacious, so alive and alight. What had happened? Was Simon back? What else could have made her so happy? She hugged him and whispered in his ear to come and talk to her, she had something to tell him. She pulled him into the snug bar and sat beside him, then told him about her baby, hers and Simon's baby. He was immediately thrilled for her and before she could ask the question he said:

"I can't tell you where he is, I don't know. He didn't tell me exactly where he was going. He will call me when he's coming back."

Her face fell, he held her close and hugged her. He desperately wanted to comfort her, he'd bent the truth somewhat, but he really didn't know where Simon currently was. He would wait until Felicity confirmed she was pregnant. He would know that tomorrow, she had promised to tell him after she returned from Plymouth. Then he would call Simon and tell him he was desperately needed back in the village.

Twenty-Two

The following day Felicity was at the cottage early, waiting for Abe and the lads to arrive. They had decided between them that they would surprise her by laying a path from the kitchen to the summerhouse Simon had built. Also, they would build a patio all round it and dig the herb garden. Abe was beaming with delight at their plans knowing how much she would appreciate it.

Seeing her waiting by the kitchen door, he went across to her and she handed him a piece of card with the name of the cottage written on it. As he looked at the card he thought to himself, *so that's the way it is.* He, as others, had suspected there was something between Felicity and Simon, it was the way they looked at each other, you could almost see the sparks. He looked again at the card, SIMON'S FEL. It was a good name and would look lovely on the gate. Rustic style, he thought, in keeping with the whole cottage. She was animatedly talking to Stan and Dave. As Abe watched her, she subconsciously and tenderly stroked her stomach with her hands. He had seen his Jeannie do that with a special smile on her face each time she had been pregnant. He smiled widely, he would say nothing but he felt so inordinately pleased for her. Good grief, he was getting romantic in his old age!

"Come on lads," he said briskly, "we have work to do." Smiling hugely at her, Abe ushered his lads off to their tasks and Felicity left to go on her own errands. First the test kit, then the chairs and a table, then she would fetch the painting. It took her nearly all day to find the furniture she wanted but eventually she found everything. The store owner loaded them into her Land Rover and she set off for the workshop to get her painting. As she went inside, she frowned. She was sure she'd left the chairs under the works stations but one was in the middle of the floor. Strange, she must have forgotten it. She dismissed the thought and concentrated on why she was there. She frowned again as she stood by the easel. Where had that cupboard come from? It hadn't been there yesterday. Who on earth had placed it in the workshop? She opened it and gasped as she saw the shelves and drawers arranged neatly side by side. She opened the drawers and smiled as she saw the trays neatly arranged to hold brushes and pens, pastel crayons and all other manner of equipment needed for her art and craft classes. She closed the cupboard and decided it must have been Lucy and Michael who had found it for her. Who else could have done so? Not Simon, he had gone away so it had to be them. She would thank them later. She turned back to the easel and took the sheet off the painting. After carefully wrapping it in paper, she carried it to the car and then made her way back to the cottage with her treasures.

Simon watched her leave the workshop, he had hidden himself behind the church wall opposite. No-one knew he had come back. He hadn't gone to France, he had stayed at his friend's farm, finishing the last item for Felicity's workshop. He'd wanted to put the final piece of furniture there as a surprise for her. He'd moved the easel to put the cupboard in place and as he did so, the sheet fell off. He was astonished to see himself, it was an excellent painting of him. Felicity had captured him perfectly; it was like looking in a mirror. Entranced he had grabbed a chair and sat down to study it; how long he sat there he didn't know. Common sense suddenly came to mind, he must get away, Felicity could come at any time and he musn't be seen here. Quickly putting the easel back and covering the painting, he left as he had entered, by the back door.

As he crossed the road to go back through the churchyard to where he had left his car, he heard the sound of her car engine so he waited, wanting to see her. He clenched his fists and dug his hands deep into his pockets. He knew that if he didn't he wouldn't be able to stop himself from running across the road and taking her in his arms. As she got out of the car his breath caught in his throat. She looked beautiful; there was a light about her, she was smiling and it lit her whole face. He groaned, his legs started to shake, he couldn't move. He realised just how much he loved her, how much he had missed her. He watched as she went up into the workshop and waited until she came out. She was carrying what could only be the painting. As she drove off he caught a glimpse of the chairs in the Land Rover and reasoned she was on her way to the cottage.

He decided he would phone Ray that night.

Twenty-Three

When Felicity arrived at the cottage, Abe, Stan and Dave were waiting for her. She was surprised they were still there, normally they would have gone home by this time as dusk was now approaching. Abe took her arm and led her round to the summerhouse, the two lads following. They stood and waited nervously for her reaction. She couldn't believe what they had done. A big pink bow had been attached to the summerhouse door. A large sign had been pinned to the door with the words 'For Miss Felicity, who has made our job so enjoyable and happy'. Then she noticed the path that led from the summerhouse to the kitchen door and the lovely curved patio going right round the summerhouse. Abe was guiding her gently to the back of the kitchen where they had dug the herb garden, neatly edged and ready for planting. She was overwhelmed, they had been so kind and it all looked so right for the cottage.

Tears again. She seemed to be crying frequently lately, but she was feeling really emotional. She hugged each one of them in turn and told them they must all come to the party she was planning when she moved in. They must bring their wives or girlfriends or whoever. They all laughed at her excitement and accepted her invitation with delight. Abe declared his Jeannie would be absolutely thrilled at the chance of going to a party! The two boys, happy at the thought of a party were already discussing who they might take. Finally Abe produced the cottage sign. It was beautiful, the letters were carved into a lovely piece of oak, still edged with bark and varnished to a high gloss. All he had to do was fix it to the gate. She asked him to do this for her first thing on the 1 December, the day she was moving in, not before, which he happily agreed to do. Then just as they were about to leave, he spotted the chairs and table in her car.

"Come on boys, we'll put these in the cottage for Miss Felicity. Where do you want them?"

He directed this last comment to Felicity and she told him they were all to go in the small bedroom, her sitting room. They happily obliged and then Abe asked about the painting. He carried it up to her sitting room for her and offered to hang it on the wall. She smiled and said that was one job she wanted to do herself. He pecked her on the cheek, gave her a big hug and left. It was only a few days now and she would move in.

Finally alone, she took out the test kit and diligently followed the instructions, impatiently waiting and watching for the tell tale colour change. She then smiled and cried simultaneously when her suspicions were confirmed; the test had proved that she was pregnant.

She was having a baby, Simon's baby. She was so ecstatic and happy she danced round her sitting room then picked up the phone to call Ray as she had promised. She dialled his number and when he answered, still crying with happiness all she could say was:

"We're having a baby." Ray smiled as she cut the call off then his smile disappeared as he went to look up Simon's number. He needed to call him and tell him he must come back, but not why. It wasn't for him to give Simon that news. Ten minutes later, frustrated that he hadn't been able to get Simon, his own phone rang.

"Yes!" he barked.

"Ray, it's Simon, I need to see you, can you meet me at Felicity's workshop in half an hour?"

Twenty-Four

Surprised, Ray immediately agreed and set off straight away, although he would be early. He sat in his car outside the workshop waiting for Simon, thinking of the news about the baby. He was really happy for Felicity, but worried about Simon's reaction when he found out, which would not be through him. A few moments later, Ray saw Simon waving at him from the churchyard. Smiling at the intrigue, Ray left his car and went across to meet him. They shook hands and Ray was surprised to notice that Simon was shaking and he looked thinner, he had certainly lost weight. Suddenly he turned and walked off through the churchyard with Ray following closely. They reached Simon's car and both men got in. Silence loomed but Ray waited for Simon to state why he had wanted this meeting.

Taking a deep breath, he began, his hands still shaking as he gripped the steering wheel.

"I know you are fully aware of my background and I know that Felicity does not know of it. I overheard her say when she saw her mother, that she wanted nothing to do with the James family after the way my half-brother had treated her. In fact, her actual words were that she wished them all in hell!" Ray raised his eyebrows at this, it seemed so out of character for Felicity. Simon continued:

"I have decided to tell her who I really am, she deserves to know, there shouldn't be any secrets between us, and I will take the consequences of that however painful and difficult that may turn out to be." He paused and clenched his hands together to stop them shaking, then turned to look at Ray as he stated:

"I am deeply in love with her Ray, no other woman has ever got right into my heart and soul as she has. I think you know somehow that we spent a night together at the cottage, one I will never forget. It completely changed my life. I know she felt the same, I know that for sure. But will she still feel the same when she finds out who I am? I feel I cannot live without her, but if it means that being with her would make her unhappy, then I will go away and love her from afar." His voice was anguished. Ray could hear the pain in it at the thought of losing Felicity. He could understand that pain, he had felt it; still did at times since he had lost Katherine.

Simon couldn't speak, he was visibly trembling and Ray knew he was at breaking point. He had always respected Simon, sometimes they disagreed but they'd always had a mutual respect for each other. Ray was sad for Simon, he was a good man, prone to temper outbursts but nothing more. He knew in his heart that these two should be together. He remembered how he had felt the first time he and Katherine had made love together, it had rocked him to the core of his soul and he could understand Simon's deep torment. The bond between Simon and Felicity was too strong to be broken by past happenings that should not affect the present. Life was too short to be hampered in such a way.

Ray thought for a while and then suggested a path that Simon may wish to follow. He didn't want to intrude on their lives, but perhaps a little advice might help him make his decision. Simon listened to what Ray had to say. He started to relax, then finally smiled as he agreed that Ray's advice was sound. They parted as friends, then as Ray started to get out of Simon's car, he turned back and said quietly:

"If Felicity would like me to, I would be happy to give her away to you with all my blessings."

Twenty-Five

It was 1 December. It seemed the whole village had turned up at the pub for Felicity's party to celebrate her move to Simon's Fel. Abe had fixed the sign to the gate early that morning, proud and pleased with the result of his efforts. As he walked away from the cottage, he turned to look at it with a critical eye. He was pleased, very pleased with the end result. It looked lovely in the winter sun, the new thatch had a glow as the sun shone across it. Everything was neat and clean, Simon's efforts in the garden had given it a real country cottage look. A good job he decided, one they could all be proud of. He would remember to tell Stan and Dave how pleased he was with the work they had done. He went off home to help Jeannie get the children ready for the party; it was going to be a good day.

Lucy and Michael had insisted that the party be held at the pub and during the morning, she had helped Felicity move all her personal belongings from there to the cottage. While they were busy putting her bits and pieces where Felicity wanted them many of the villagers turned up with gifts for her. Jams and pickles, cakes and bread, eggs and even a chicken, thankfully ready for the oven! Homemade wine and Sloe Gin were brought, fresh vegetables and preserved fruit followed. The butcher came along with fresh meat for her freezer and someone had thought to put a vase of fresh flowers in each room. Lucy and Jeannie between them had managed to put these in the night before, using the key to the cottage that Abe still had. Jeannie would return it to her today at the party.

Felicity had enough provisions to last her quite a while. Several times she burst into tears as more gifts came. Frequently she excused herself and rushed to the bathroom, morning sickness troubling her just a bit. Several of the village women looked at each other and nodded wisely, guessing the reason for her sudden disappearances. They well remembered that feeling and look from their own experiences.

Shaking and a bit pale, she did as told and went back to the pub for the party lunch Michael had prepared. As they left the cottage to return to the pub, Felicity noticed several pots of plants along her path. She turned to Lucy to ask where they had come from. Anticipating her question, Lucy just said that several villagers thought she might like some plants to start her flower and herb gardens.

Ray had talked to Lucy and Michael telling them of his meeting with Simon, not the details, just the important information. He wanted them to try and keep

Felicity from the cottage in the afternoon, hence the lunch party. The villagers were helping this along even though they were unaware of exactly why this was happening. Abe and Jeannie and their two little ones were there. Dave and Stan had brought their girlfriends. The villagers had turned out in full; it was turning into a real party. The pub was crowded, but everyone was in high spirits. Lucy and Michael had hung up banners saying 'Good Luck In Your New Home' and music was playing in the background. Even Felicity, although slightly shaky and tired, began to enjoy the atmosphere and join in with the fun. Customers who were strangers to the village got drawn into the happy atmosphere of the party.

One thought that could not be dismissed by Felicity was that Simon wasn't there. She had so hoped he would be; had convinced herself that he would turn up. Suddenly the thought flashed across her mind – the painting – she hadn't hung it in her sitting room. It had to be there, she must find Ray and get him to take her to the cottage to put it up.

Lucy and Michael told Felicity that Ray would be there soon when she asked where he was. They wouldn't let her leave and kept her occupied with meeting all the villagers in turn. It was a happy day but exhausting and Felicity was getting very tired, she wanted to get to her cottage. It was just after five and Lucy, ever watchful, saw her looking round for Ray, so went over to engage Felicity in conversation. Quietly she said to her that if she needed any help with anything, anything at all, she must ask them and, by the way, she knew a good midwife.

Having caught Felicity's full attention with this statement they laughed and hugged and made silly plans for the baby. Ray at last appeared. It was now nearly six, he winked at Lucy who immediately steered Felicity towards him.

"I think we have kept Felicity from her new home for long enough Ray, take her home." Ten minutes later, goodbyes said, Ray walked Felicity to Simon's Fel. She so loved the name, it was so right and she loved the cottage. If only Simon were here.

"Ray," she started, a stricken look on her face. He held her hand tightly and smiled at her.

"Don't worry, don't think, just go and sit quietly in your sitting room, please. There is a surprise in there for you. Just go straight there." He patted her hand, guided her through the door and kissed her gently on her cheek. He gestured at the staircase motioning her to go up and left, inordinately pleased with himself.

Somewhat amused and intrigued Felicity made her way up the stairs and into her sitting room. Her hand flew to her mouth as she opened the door and she clutched at the handle to stop herself from falling. Simon was standing in the room holding a piece of paper in one hand, his other clenched tight round something. Her painting had been hung over the fireplace, it looked superb, but who had put it there? Simon's heart flipped over when he saw Felicity, she looked tired but so lovely. He had to steel himself not to rush across and kiss her. He had missed her so much; he should never have left her. Mentally he shook himself and said:

"Felicity, sit down before you fall down, I have something important to say to you."

She automatically did as she was bid and thankfully sank into the chair, her brain could not fathom this situation. Simon took a deep breath and launched into his tale:

"Felicity, this will be a shock to you, but you need to know about me. This is my birth certificate. My father was your father-in-law. Your late husband was my half-brother. I have changed my name to Grantley, the surname of the lady who owned this cottage. She was my grandmother and I am her sole direct descendant. I am deeply in love with you. I want you for my wife. I want us to have our baby together. This ring belonged to Grace, I found it in her box. Felicity, will you please marry me?"

He came across to her, dropped his certificate on the floor, knelt down in front of her and opened his clenched hand. The ring was beautiful, delicate with small diamonds surrounding a deep red ruby. He lifted her chin so she could see into his eyes. Smoky grey, silver lights glinting, his deep desire for her so obvious as his eyes darkened. He was trembling as he touched her, he wanted to crush her to him, but needed her answer first. He may yet have to go and leave her.

Everything he had said, so much yet so little, was a jumble in her mind. Her husband's half-brother, but how? So many questions she needed answers to! She put her hand against her stomach, Simon wanted their baby, he wanted her, he wanted a life together with her and their child, and he loved her! She had known it but now he had told her, she could feel him shaking. Her own body started to tremble in response to the look in his beautiful eyes.

"Felicity." His anguished voice cut across her thoughts, "Felicity darling, will you, will you marry me?"

She couldn't speak, tears welled in her eyes and trickled down her cheeks, but as he reached out to her, she pushed him away and stood up.

"I can't Simon, I can't, I can't think. I have to think, please go away, please just go away!" Her voice was rising, hysteria not far away. Her breathing was fast and shallow, her heart thumping. She ran out of the door and fled to her bedroom, fell onto her bed and lay there sobbing in anguish and despair. Her heart and soul felt as though they were breaking in to pieces.

Twenty-Six

Simon rocked back on his heels at Felicity's words, shocked into silence and immobility. He heard her bedroom door close. He wanted to go to her, comfort and hold her but his head over-ruled his heart, he knew she would not want him there. Slowly he stood up still clutching the ring in his hand. Tears welled in his eyes; he had lost her, she wouldn't or couldn't marry him. He sat in her chair trying to control his shaking limbs, trying not to give in to the tears trickling down his face.

He looked up at the painting, it was such an excellent piece of work, it was the only picture their baby would have of its father. He groaned harshly and bit his lip hard to stop himself from breaking down completely. Blood trickled down his chin, but still he clamped his teeth on his lip, his heart was breaking. He had never felt such anguish and pain. *Oh God*, he thought, *how can I live without her, how can I go on in my life without her next to me?* How long he sat there, he didn't know. Finally he got up and went from the cottage, steeling himself not to throw open her bedroom door and take her in his arms. He could hear her crying, she sounded so distressed. He groaned again, his hurt and heartache turning into anger. Anger at himself; at his wretched family; at his heritage and at the circumstances that had brought them together and now ripped them apart. He found himself outside the pub, the lights were still on and there were cars in the car park. He glanced at his watch, it was nearly eleven o'clock, the pub would be closing soon. He walked round the car park and saw Ray's car there. He would wait until he came out, he needed to speak to him urgently.

Lucy, Michael and Ray had finished clearing up. The party had been a great success, all the villagers and customers seemed to enjoy the whole event. All three were thinking and wondering how Felicity had reacted to Simon's news. They would no doubt know very soon, nothing was secret for long in the village. Ray got up and stretched, said his goodbyes to Lucy and Michael having decided that as it was now eleven twenty, he needed to go home. He went out to his car and was startled when he heard Simon's voice calling to him. Ray looked round, saw Simon and went across to him. He immediately saw how upset Simon was. He looked completely devastated and was shaking uncontrollably. Ray took hold of him and pushed him into his car. Nothing was said as Ray drove back to his apartment.

A few moments later they were in the sitting room both holding glasses containing very large whiskies. Ray waited for Simon to speak, his heart heavy, guessing from Simon's demeanour that things had not gone well.

"She won't have me Ray, she said she can't, she pushed me away and rushed to her bedroom. I left her there, she was crying so hard. It's breaking my heart to know I have lost her and our baby and I just walked away and left her there." He stopped speaking, tears were running down his cheeks, he was openly crying, his emotions and deep despair over-riding his innate masculinity.

Ray said nothing, what could he say? He was upset and so sad for both of them, they belonged together, why was life so cruel? He looked at Simon then abruptly stood up and walked across to the window. Life was cruel; but hadn't they all played a part in what was happening now? Maybe they should all have had more faith in Felicity and told her the whole story. Perhaps then she may have understood and accepted Simon for who he was and not for who his family were. They were all at fault. Simon too had been less than honest with her. He'd allowed this situation to develop, he should have told her about his right to the cottage long ago. Sighing heavily, Ray turned round, Simon was sitting with his head in his hands, not moving, just sitting there.

Ray sat down in his chair, picked up his glass and downed the whisky in one go.

"We are all to blame Simon, including you. She was so happy, now you tell me you left her sobbing. How could you leave her? If you love her as much as you profess, how could you walk away? You should have broken down her door and comforted her!" His voice was harsh and Simon looked up in surprise at this outburst from Ray. He was about to speak , then stopped as Ray exclaimed loudly:

"Just what are you going to do Simon? Are you intending to disappear again? Are you going to walk away and leave her alone knowing she is having your baby? Have you no guts man?" Ray was angry at Simon, at himself, he felt so ashamed of the way they had all treated Felicity. "Incidentally, just how did you find out Felicity is pregnant?"

Simon took a few deep breaths, his temper rising at Ray's words. He too gulped his whisky down, then stood up and faced Ray.

"Some of what you say is true, I am not proud of what I have done. But you are wrong about one thing. I do love her, she is my life, I want to be with her. But *she* has rejected *me*. I have to live with that." He walked towards the door, went to go out then stopped and turned round. Still with his hand on the door, he looked directly at Ray and said:

"I want you to do something for me. I want you to arrange with your solicitor friend to have the deeds of the cottage signed over to Felicity and our baby in perpetuity. I want it to be watertight that no-one can ever get hold of the cottage, it has to be just for Felicity, the baby and their descendants. I will not fight her for it; I don't want any loopholes that could allow any of my family to be able to lay claim to it. I don't want the cottage any more. The only way I would take it is to share it with Felicity and our baby. Right now, I cannot see any solution to make that happen. Can you do this for me?"

Surprised at this turn of events, Ray hesitated then

nodded in agreement. Simon moved to open the door and Ray quickly got up, went across to him and put a hand on his shoulder to stop him leaving.

"I have to know where you are going Simon, there will be documents to sign. I must also make you aware that if you sign those papers, there will be no redress, you cannot then change it."

Simon sighed heavily, looked at Ray and stated flatly:

"I won't be far away. I will let you know exactly where I am in a couple of days. In the meantime, you have my mobile number. I have made up my mind, I will not go back on it." He opened the door but turned round again and quietly stated:

"I found out Felicity was pregnant by sheer chance. I happened to be in the chemist in Plymouth. I was close behind her in the queue and saw her purchase the test kit. She looked so glowing and happy. I just put two and two together. She looks so beautiful, she has a radiance about her. I have seen that glow in other pregnant women. I know for certain Ray, that the baby is mine."

He left, his only thought as he walked through the village was of Felicity and how cowardly he had been in leaving her. He knew the reason; he couldn't face rejection, especially from her. He'd thought she was the one person who really wanted him. All his life he had been rejected, no-one had ever shown him real love. How could he face her again knowing she had turned him away, he couldn't bear it. What if he went back and she sent him away again? Despair and desolation washed over him.

Twenty-Seven

Ray sat for a while after Simon had left, wondering how this mess could ever be sorted out. He shook his head to clear his mind and glanced at the clock. It was well after one o'clock, but he knew he would not sleep if he went to bed. He got up and went down to his office. He switched on his desk lamp, then went to the filing cabinet and found the papers relating to the cottage.

He sat at his desk and stared at the picture of Katherine. How he wished she was here at this moment, she would have known how to deal with all this. In reality, she would have put them all straight before it got this far! She would have found a way of telling Felicity about Simon's heritage and not kept it from her. She would certainly have been angry with them all for keeping it from her. Sighing heavily, he opened the file and was just starting to leaf through it when his doorbell rang. Who on earth could it be at this hour? Felicity! She must be in trouble! He went to the door fearing the worst. Simon stood there looking wretched.

Ray ushered him in wondering what had brought him back so soon.

"There is something else I need you to look after for me Ray, there is no-one else I can ask." Simon had launched into this statement almost before Ray had closed the door. He motioned Simon to a chair and waited for him to explain. Silence ensued for a few moments, then Simon drew a small box from his pocket and passed it to Ray.

"In this box is a ring that belonged to Grace, my grandmother. I wanted Felicity to have it, but that didn't happen. I want you to keep it for her Ray. It is hers, it is a symbol of my love for her. Please keep it safe for me, for Felicity."

"Surely you should keep it Simon? You should give it to her when the right moment comes along, I am sure she would understand given a little time."

"Not now Ray, not right now. I have to get something out of my system, I need to sort my thoughts out. I have allowed my despicable family to colour my life and my judgement. I cannot give to Felicity what she deserves until I rid myself of this burden my family has become, the burden I have allowed them to become. I will go to her when I am free of them all and can be the man she deserves."

Astonished, Ray could only stare at Simon. That was quite a speech. He couldn't think of anything to say in reply. He closed his hands around the box, got up and locked it in his safe. Simon stood up to leave and as he reached the door he turned to Ray.

"I am going to be with my friends at the farm so I will be close by. You know where that is, you can contact me or come and see me at anytime, for any reason. If you think Felicity needs to know, I will trust your judgement on that."

The door closed behind Simon and Ray stood looking at it, not moving for a while as the events of the last few hours trawled through his mind. He had some serious work to do on the cottage deeds, he just hoped he was right in his instincts that it could be done. First though, he must get some sleep, it was approaching two o'clock in the morning and he suddenly felt very tired.

He went back to his desk and once more studied the photo of his wife. How he missed her. Tonight especially, he needed her comfort and counselling. He promised himself that he would tell Felicity tomorrow, well today actually, about the cottage. Just how he would do that, he didn't know. But; no more secrets. That had led to enough heartache already.

Twenty-Eight

Lucy and Jeannie were becoming very concerned about Felicity; she wasn't eating and although she went to the workshop, her heart was not in her work and she had cancelled her classes. It was two weeks since Felicity had moved to the cottage, she looked pale and thin, rarely went out and she didn't want to talk. Lucy had decided to bully her into seeing the doctor, at least to plan for the baby, she hadn't yet been to meet the midwife or gone to ante-natal classes. *Damn*, thought Lucy, how was she going to persuade her?

Felicity had got up that same morning and had been shocked at her appearance when she looked in the mirror. She was pale and haggard; had lost weight and was feeling quite ill and very tired. She sat in the kitchen cradling her cup of coffee wondering what she could do to get back to some semblance of well-being. The baby! She had almost forgotten about it in her deep unhappiness and total sense of loss. She put her cup down and went upstairs to her bedroom. She undressed and looked at herself critically in the full length mirror. There was a slight swelling to her stomach and she ran her hands over the small but perceptible bump. How selfish she had been wallowing in her own misery and putting her baby at risk. She must take care of herself for the baby's sake. She put her hands protectively on her swelling stomach and for the first time since that awful night, a weak smile played on her lips. She would go and see Lucy, get some advice from her, but first she must see Ray about the cottage. She knew it was Simon's by right, he must have it, she must find somewhere else to live, somewhere for her and the baby; Ray would help her find something. She would not allow herself to think about Simon, it was too painful, she had shut the door on the painting and had not been in that room since that night.

For the first time in two weeks Felicity had some purpose, she left the cottage and went directly to Ray's office. He was surprised but very pleased to see her as all attempts to visit her had been firmly refused. He was concerned about her appearance though as she was very pale, thin and looked gaunt. She managed a weak smile and launched into her reason for being there. She didn't get very far into her explanation before Ray interrupted her to tell her that she was too late, Simon had decided to sign the deeds over to her. She protested vehemently and told Ray to stop the procedure.

"It's too late Felicity," Ray said. "Simon signed the papers yesterday, it is done, it is final, it cannot be reversed. You cannot ever sell it on to anyone as it is for your baby in perpetuity." He stopped as Felicity sagged back into the chair, tears streaming down her face, her hands gently stroking her modest bump.

"Our baby," she said, "he loves our baby." She was crying, almost sobbing but smiling at the same time. It lifted Ray's spirits, just to see her smile, he would let Simon know; he deserved that.

Calm now, Felicity listened as Ray told her that as soon as the deeds arrived, he would give her a copy and keep the originals in his safe. She nodded, having admitted defeat as far as Simon's Fel was concerned. She was still so confused. She had picked up Simon's birth certificate from where he had dropped it. There was no doubt about his lineage, she just couldn't bring herself to see him as an individual. She could only think of him as the half-brother of her late husband, that dreadful, violent and cruel man. She must go and think, she had to sort it out, she couldn't go on in this state of limbo. She must make up her mind about Simon. She drew her breath in sharply and her eyes shone as her treacherous mind reminded her of the joy they had shared together and of just how much she loved him. Ray watched the changing expressions on her face, ready to help her if she became upset again. She stood up suddenly and smiled at Ray saying:

"I'm going to see Lucy, then I'm going home to think."

Lucy hugged her when she arrived at the pub, so relieved to see her out and about. Jeannie was there, having called in to ask Lucy if she had seen Felicity lately;

she too had been worried for her and the baby. They were both concerned with her wan appearance, but became less so when Felicity asked for advice about the baby, what she needed to do and when. By the time she left to go home, appointments had been made with the doctor, midwife and the ante-natal clinic. She had also welcomed the help Lucy and Jeannie offered with preparing the nursery in the New Year. No-one had mentioned Simon by name but as soon as Felicity had left, Michael and Lucy wondered where he was and if he knew how Felicity was doing. They resolved to ask Ray.

The news about the cottage was relayed to Lucy and Michael when Ray went for lunch at the pub later that day. They were surprised but pleased that at last the matter of the cottage had been settled. Lucy immediately asked Ray where Simon was and did he know how Felicity was and of course the baby? Ray just quietly stated that Simon was ok, he knew about Felicity and that was all he was prepared to say. Michael opened his mouth to protest, but Lucy stopped him. Knowing her brother so well, she knew that he would not say anymore until he was ready.

As Felicity approached the cottage her heart stopped, there was a police car parked outside and her immediate thought was Simon. *Oh my God!* Her mind whirled round, her legs buckled and she fell to the ground, banging her head on the pavement and losing consciousness. The two policemen rushed to help her, one already on his phone calling the local doctor, who agreed to come out immediately. They carefully picked her up and carried her to their car, tenderly laying her on the back seat. She moaned and stirred, opening her eyes to see two anxious faces staring at her. The doctor arrived just as Felicity was handing her door keys to the policemen. They insisted on carrying her in, the doctor following behind. He immediately gestured them upstairs where they laid her on her bed and the doctor quickly examined her. He decided she was not concussed just shaken. Felicity shyly told him she was pregnant and anxiously asked if her baby was alright. The doctor asked her a few questions and examined her again, then declared the baby was fine. She must just rest and come to see him the next day to make sure she was ok, and by the way, had she booked in with the midwife and the ante-natal clinic. Felicity confirmed that was all arranged and the doctor left saying he would see her the next day.

"Why are you here?" she suddenly asked the policemen, colour draining from her face once again.

"We have some rather sad news Miss Huntley." The older of the two officers took hold of her hand. "I'm afraid your mother has died."

Twenty-Nine

Felicity's immediate reaction to this news was relief, then surprise.

"But she wasn't ill!" she said to the officer. "What happened?"

Patiently they explained that a neighbour had been concerned that they hadn't seen her for a couple of days. She was so habitual in what she did they knew something must be wrong. The police were called, they broke into the house and discovered her in bed, she had died in her sleep and a post-mortem proved she had suffered a massive heart attack. It had happened a week ago, and it had taken the police since then to track her down from papers and notes they had found in her mother's bureau. They had also discovered a will, now with the solicitor.

Lucy arrived at the cottage, the grapevine having done its work. The two police officers left, happy to go now that Felicity was not alone and had a friend to look to her needs. She related the story to Lucy who immediately said she would accompany Felicity to London to sort everything out. It was such a busy time of the year, Christmas was only two weeks away. Should they go now or wait until New Year? They decided to go immediately, they could arrange everything in a couple of days and Michael could manage for that time, Lucy firmly stating that Ray would lend a hand if necessary.

Next day they were on the midday train to London. They arrived late afternoon at the house and just as Felicity had expected, her mother had left everything in order. The whole house was clean and tidy and all her papers were neatly filed in the bureau. Felicity quickly phoned the solicitor before his office closed for the day to find out about the will. He briefly explained that her mother had left the house to Felicity, and the rest of her estate was to be donated to her favourite charity. Felicity was not interested in the details so she informed the solicitor to liase with the estate agent who would be dealing with the sale of the house and to just send her the proceeds when the property was sold. The funeral was arranged for the second week in January, the Christmas period and New Year delaying things. Lucy gently asked Felicity if she wanted to go and see her mother but she declined, she had no emotional feelings of any sort for the woman who had treated her so badly. She would do the necessary for her as she would for anyone else, but that was all. They had arranged for a house clearance firm to deal with the contents, all the clothes were collected by the Salvation Army and the house details were given to an estate agent along with a set of house keys. The agent had been instructed to sell the property without any negotiation with Felicity, she was not interested, she just wanted to be rid of it and the bad memories it held. All that remained were her mother's personal papers, so they boxed these up to take back to Devon to be dealt with. The attic, thought Felicity, we haven't looked in the attic. Together, she and Lucy opened the hatch, unhooked the ladder and went to see what had been put up there.

Not much, thought Felicity as she looked round. A couple of old chairs were stacked against the rafters and an old trunk was pushed under the eaves. Lucy dragged it out and pushed it into the middle of the attic floor. Felicity was surprised, it was her father's, his initials were on the lid, she remembered it from when she was very small, her father had kept his old army bits and pieces in there.

Excited, she opened it only to be disappointed. There was nothing in there except one envelope that looked relatively new and clean. Intrigued, Felicity picked it up and turned it over only to gasp out loud as she saw her name written on it. Her Father had written 'For Felicity on the event of my death'. Why hadn't she been given this? How had it got into the trunk? Who had put it there? The answers to all these questions came to Felicity in a flash. Her mother! Her mother had hidden it! Her father had been dead for nine years, and her mother must have hidden this at the time of his death. But why? Felicity ripped open the envelope and read the sheet that was enclosed.

My Dear Felicity,

I am writing this in the hope that you will understand and I pray that you will live your life as you want. I should never have married your mother, all she wanted was someone to mould into who she thought was suitable for her selfish needs. When she realised she couldn't change me as she wanted, she was determined to have a child. I will not tell that story, but sufficient to say that after she became pregnant with you, that side of our life, such as it was, stopped completely. I was no saint, I admit I sought solace elsewhere; it was the one and only joy in my life outside of my relationship with you. I loved you, my special daughter. Your mother tried to recreate you into her image and the only reason I stayed in the marriage was to hopefully prevent her from succeeding in her goal. Finally, I could stand no more, I was truly alone as my friend (who gave me happiness) passed away. Before I leave and go, one more thing Felicity, if you find the chance of happiness, knowing in your heart and soul that this person is the one you want to be with, knowing it is true love you feel, then take it, don't let it go, don't miss the chance of being with and loving that person. Remember, the only things in life that you regret are the risks you don't take. Be safe and happy Felicity.

Your everloving Dad.

Felicity passed the sheet to Lucy, she was too choked with emotion to speak. Oh how she wished she had known about this letter after her father had died, it would have saved her so much heartache and unhappiness. She cried again, this time for her father; tears of pride and love for him. Tears of joy for him that he had at least found some comfort in his life through his 'friend'. The letter had brought tears to Lucy's eyes and they cried together before they went out of the loft, closed it all up and prepared to return to Devon.

Felicity was very quiet on the way home. Lucy didn't bother her, just let her think her own thoughts and adjust to the happenings of the last few days. They arrived back home to snow on the ground and a feeling of festivity around the village. Tired, the two women went their separate ways and as Felicity went into her cottage, she noticed that someone had been in and kept the Aga alight and some Christmas decorations had been put up in the hall. It looked lovely, so welcoming and she wondered who had done this? Ray, she decided, she would go and see him tomorrow to thank him. Now, she just wanted to go to bed. The emotional turmoil of the past few weeks had caught up with her and she was physically, mentally and emotionally exhausted. Her last thought before sleep claimed her was of Simon, how she loved him and what they had lost.

She shot up from the bed, her eyes wide open and a huge smile on her face. Dad, oh Dad, she thought, you clever, wonderful man.

Thirty

As soon as she woke next morning, Felicity jumped out of bed. She knew just what she was going to do and the thought made her heart leap and her nerve ends tingle. She was singing as she bustled about in the kitchen, the village postman smiling as he heard her, happy that she was in good spirits, she had been so sad of late. She spent the next couple of hours putting Christmas decorations around the sitting rooms and draping some up the stairway. Pleased with her efforts, she went outside and noticed that her driveway and path had been cleared of snow. Someone had been busy, surely not Ray, probably Lucy and Michael's son Justin, now home from university for the Christmas break. She must remember to thank him.

Back indoors, she showered, letting the water course down over her body, revelling in the softness of it as she closed her eyes and remembered the feel of Simon's caresses. Her legs trembled as she allowed herself to feel her memories. Quickly she turned the shower off before her thoughts went too far.

Smiling happily, she dressed warmly then made her way to the surgery to see the doctor and midwife, her appointments having been delayed by the trip to London. She was well they pronounced, both of them in turn pleased to see her smiling and looking radiant. Her scan was booked at the hospital, she was given her due date and the midwife gave her all the booklets and information she needed for the birth of the baby. There was a lot to read through, but she was happily looking forward to preparing the cottage for the new arrival. Early June; a summer baby, it was going to be a good year.

She sang quietly as she walked along to see Ray, she had some very important questions to ask him and she was not leaving until she got the answers. She would take her father's advice, take her chance, live her life being alive and alight with the man she loved. Her eyes were shining and happiness was emanating from her as she walked into Ray's office. He was astounded at how different Felicity looked, she was positively radiant. Had she seen Simon? he thought. No, she couldn't have, she didn't know where he was and he hadn't been to the village since he'd signed the papers.

"Ray, where is Simon? I need to see him, it's urgent. Please tell me where he is."

"Sit down Felicity," Ray replied, "and tell me why you need to know?"

"Advice from my father. Ray, please read this, I think it will explain everything."

Ray took the sheet of paper from Felicity and after he

had read it, he gave it back to her and smiled, a happy beaming smile. Thank God, he thought, thank God for Felicity's father. He got up from his chair, went across to his safe and returned with a small package.

"Before you see Simon, I think you should have this, it will tell Simon all he needs to know." Ray handed the package to Felicity. He wanted to dance round the room, he felt so happy for these two people of whom he had become so fond.

She frowned at Ray's cryptic remark and took the package from his outstretched hand. She opened it, and gasped as she recognised what she was holding. She looked up at Ray who was still standing in front of her. Smiling and crying at the same time she said:

"You knew, you knew all along, yet you said nothing. Why?"

Ray took hold of Felicity's hands and pulled her up from the chair. He put his arms around her, hugging her tightly and said:

"Simon asked me to give you this when I thought the time was right, I think that time is now. Go home Felicity, I will ring Simon and tell him you need to see him. He will come."

He shooed her out of his office then rang Simon. As soon as he answered his phone Ray said:

"Felicity needs to see you, she has the ring."

He rang off before Simon could say anything and feeling extremely pleased, he locked his office, put a note on the door saying he was at a festive lunch and went to see Lucy and Michael. He decided he would not return to work that day, he would celebrate. He would tell Lucy and Michael why he was there and they would celebrate together,

Thirty minutes later, Simon arrived at the cottage. He was shaking, hoping he had correctly interpreted the message from Ray. The kitchen door was unlocked and as he went through to the hall, he could hear Felicity singing softly, her voice coming from upstairs. His heart lurched, he knew where she would be. He took the stairs two at a time and went into her small sitting room. He stopped just inside the door; she looked beautiful, radiant. She was glowing, smiling, and her eyes were alight with joy. She was stroking her stomach, the small bump that was their baby.

She was watching him, her eyes looking directly into his, those incredible silver specks were glinting, the smoky greyness darkening as he saw the involuntary response in her own eyes.

"Simon," she said softly, her voice husky as she held out her hand, the ring on her wedding finger. "I should have said yes to you when you asked me before, I am saying yes now. Have I left it too late?"

Simon walked across the room and knelt down in front of her. He put his hands gently on her stomach, all the while looking deep into her eyes, his own smouldering with fire, his body trembling as he saw the answering fire in her own eyes. He smiled as he gently caressed her stomach. He couldn't speak, his happiness was so great. He gathered her into his arms and drew her up from the chair. She fell against him, her body moulding itself into his. For a long time he just held her in his arms, shaking as he revelled in the feel of her so close to him; a solace to his desire and need for her, taking away the hurt and grief of the past few weeks. She moaned into his chest, her body telling him how much she wanted him. He lifted her up and carried her into the bedroom, their love almost lighting up the room.

Thirty-One

Little Trenchard celebrated two very happy events in the New Year. First was the wedding.

Simon and Felicity were married in the village church in early March. Ray beamed with pride as he walked Felicity down the aisle. Abe and Jeannie smiled with delight as Bella trotted after Felicity as her bridesmaid. Lucy was proudest of all as Matron of Honour. She had been overwhelmed when Felicity had asked her, thrilled to do so for this lovely young woman who had become such a good friend. Michael had been astonished when Simon had asked him to be his best man. He was delighted to accept and happy to provide the wedding breakfast for Simon and Felicity as their wedding present to them. It truly was a great day and the wedding party carried on for hours. The whole village had been invited; it was a really happy event.

Three months later, the village celebrated again when Felicity and Simon's baby was born; a boy who they named James after Felicity's father.

Abe had secretly made a small sign to add to the one he had made for Felicity when she moved to the cottage. All he had to do was add the baby's name. The morning after James was born, he hung it on the gate alongside 'Simon's Fel'. It simply said 'And James'.

Acknowledgements

My eternal thanks to Katie Bosworth for editing my first draft, her invaluable help and for encouraging me to persevere to complete my book.

My grateful thanks to Kari McGowan MA for producing the wonderful artwork for my book cover.